Please return on or before the latest date above.
You can renew online at *www.kent.gov.uk/libs*
or by telephone 08458 247 200

CUSTOMER SERVICE EXCELLENCE

Libraries & Archives

00884\DTP\RN\07.07   LIB 7

HOW DOES YOUR GARDEN GROW?

Lyn Jolley

CHIVERS

British Library Cataloguing in Publication Data available

This Large Print edition published by AudioGo Ltd, Bath, 2011.
Published by arrangement with the author

U.K. Hardcover ISBN 978 1 445 83610 2
U.K. Softcover ISBN 978 1 445 83611 9

Printed and bound in Great Britain by
CPI Antony Rowe, Chippenham and Eastbourne

CHAPTER ONE

The gleaming kitchen buzzed with inhuman activity. Whilst the dishwasher thrust jets of scalding water over the breakfast crockery, the washing machine pounded lavender sheets in a fragrant, bubbling foam and the tumble dryer tossed shirts and blouses irreverently about. Caroline thought it a shame and an extravagance to dry the washing indoors on such a bright summer morning, but Clive had not wanted a clothesline to ruin the effect of their newly landscaped garden, so she had no alternative.

As she gazed out of the kitchen window at the pond, with its rampant stone fish defiantly spewing water into the air, as if in protest at its unnatural posture, Caroline sighed heavily. It had cost a not so small fortune, the conversion of the garden into a 'suburban haven'. Unfortunately, she found the end result pretentious and somehow sterile in its uniformity. The crazy paving on the spacious patio looked so neatly contrived that all sense of its promised rustic charm had been lost. The white, plastic furniture, purporting to be wrought iron, was too clinical to be welcoming. Whilst the tall, straight conifers, which formed a barrier between the Marshall's garden and the outside world, constantly reminded

Caroline of a row of inanimate sentries, which allowed her no glimpse of anything but this engineered tribute to man's vanity. Only human beings, Caroline decided, could have the audacity to take nature into their control in this way. To her, the weed-free flowerbeds, with their colour coordinated shrubs, and the neatly trimmed lawn, with not one rogue clover to be seen, represented a wilderness. She was uncertain why, but it frightened her.

* * *

Caroline sat down at the breakfast bar. She sipped her orange juice and began to think deeply about her life. This was a doubtful luxury in which she found herself indulging more and more since her only son, Adam, had gone to university.

It was a time for taking stock, she supposed. And though she was determined not to join the army of middle-aged women who flounder perilously in that huge void which appears in their lives when their young have flown the nest, Caroline knew that all was not right with her world. To identify the faults and to attempt to remedy them—so achieving peace of mind and true happiness—had become her most compelling and persistent pursuit.

The first and most obvious problem was her age. Caroline was almost forty-three. Now, although she knew that she could do nothing to alter the passage of time, what she did want to change was her attitude towards this tyrannical phenomenon. Digging a little deeper, though, was it HER attitude that troubled her? No . . . Caroline pondered . . . no, it was not. Why did she bother to have her hair tinted, and in so doing, cover up her naturally grey roots? Why did she try every new diet that came on to the market and weigh herself morning and night, praying that the little black needle would reassure her, beyond all doubt, that she had lost another six ounces? Why did she smother herself in every anti-wrinkle cream and moisturizer that she saw advertised, and allow no-one to see her until she had applied at least one layer of foundation? Clive! The answer to all these somewhat pitiful questions was that she behaved as she did because of Clive!

Her husband was only six months her junior, yet to Caroline's constant annoyance (and his own obvious satisfaction) Clive appeared to be growing more handsome with the onset of middle age. His thick, dark brown hair was somehow enhanced by the few silver strands, which now waved gently on his temples. Whilst his face was strengthened and made quite rugged by the small lines that had recently begun to chisel mature masculinity into a countenance that had previously been too perfect to show either character or worldliness.

Caroline twisted and turned in front of the

full-length mirror, which adorned the lobby of their luxurious detached house. She looked first over one shoulder and then the other. Her hips were still remarkably slim—in fact, her figure had scarcely altered since her youth. A prolonged scrutiny of her face followed and after some deliberation Caroline decided that she was wearing rather well. She had a basically good bone structure, with a jaw line that allowed femininity and strength to mingle, and cheekbones that added depth to her intense hazel eyes. Her hair, though highlighted by a titian glow, which nature had not provided, was still thick and glossy as it lay in its expensively created yet casual style.

Perhaps she had been unfair to Clive. Yes, she enjoyed looking attractive. She should not blame him for her continuing struggle against the signs of aging—the natural process, which proved so threatening to many of her sex. It was as much for her own vanity that she clung to her youthful appearance as for Clive's approval.

Occasionally, though, a transient but disconcerting desire passed across Caroline's lively mind. She wished that she could abandon all efforts to maintain a chic image, and declare to one and all that she was putting on weight and going rapidly grey, but her cautious personality would not permit such rash behaviour. Unfortunately she craved admiration . . . admiration that seemed

4

inextricably linked to an attractive exterior, so she would remain under constant self-assessment and work hard at the face that she showed to the world.

*   *   *

There was a sharp knock at the back door.

' 'Morning, Mrs. Marshall!'

'Hello, Mrs. Curran!'

'It's glorious today . . . really warm.'

'It's lovely, isn't it?'

The rotund Mrs. Curran hung her jacket in the kitchen cupboard and put on her overall.

'I'll start on the bedrooms, shall I?' she asked, dragging the vacuum cleaner behind her like a reluctant puppy dog.

'Please do!' Caroline replied, knowing that her char was out of earshot and that she would do exactly as she wished anyway.

Though Mrs. Curran only came three mornings a week to undertake the heavier cleaning work for which machines had either not been invented or still needed human assistance, Caroline felt that she should really manage the household chores on her own. Clive insisted that she should have help, though, and Mrs. Curran was cheerful company, so Caroline did not force the issue—especially as housework was not her favourite pastime.

The vacuum cleaner droned monotonously

in the rooms above as Caroline made coffee for herself and her helper.

'I've made our drink earlier than usual,' she explained as Mrs. Curran made herself as comfortable as possible on a high kitchen stool which seemed fashioned for someone with a far smaller frame than hers, 'because I'm going over to my mother's.'

'Oh, that's nice. How is she these days?'

'It's hard to say really. She worries me sometimes, I must admit.'

'Not too well then?'

'She isn't ill—not exactly. She's very overweight. I suppose that's her main problem. Then last week she had a fall.'

'Oh dear. That is nasty when you're getting on . . . it's the shock . . . you never now what it'll do. My sister, Joyce, she's only fifty-five, but she fell over on the ice last winter and broke her leg.'

'I remember you telling me.'

'Shocking break it was. I don't think it's ever healed properly. She's still got a dreadful limp and she has to use a walking stick if she goes out.'

'Mm. Mum managed to make her neighbour hear by banging on the wall . . . otherwise she might have lain there for ages.'

'Yes, of course she might . . . that is a worry for you, isn't it?'

'I'm afraid she'll fall down the stairs and knock herself unconscious or something. I often think of her late at night and wonder if she's all right.'

'Well, that's only natural. It makes me cross, you know, the way people jump to conclusions when something goes wrong with the old folk—a fall or something. They're always so ready to point the finger, to blame the children for not looking after them—but look at you—worrying yourself sick. I mean, you've got your own life to lead, haven't you?'

'Mm,' Caroline agreed unconvincingly. She felt suddenly defensive.

'I expect your mum gets a bit low, does she . . . depressed?'

'No, no she doesn't, actually. She's always been a very jolly person, my mum—very easy-going. I wish I were like her in that respect. She never grumbles.'

'Oh well, that's something to be grateful for.'

'Yes, I suppose it is.'

'My old mum never stopped moaning, bless her. Mind you, there were seven of us—a good job, too! At least we shared her out a bit . . . moaned all the blessed time, she did. My husband used to say it was the only thing that kept her going, a good moan.'

'Did he? Seven of you, were there?'

Caroline never ceased to marvel at the vastness of Mrs. Curran's family.

'How's young Alan?' the cleaner inquired cheerfully.

'Adam,' Caroline put in.

'It must be nearly time for his summer holiday, surely.'

'Yes, he comes home at the end of the month.'

'That'll be nice for you.'

'He isn't staying long.'

'Oh?'

'No, he's coming here for a long weekend—to get his washing and ironing up to date, no doubt—and then he's off to France, camping with some friends of his.'

'What, all summer?'

'For about a month, I think. Then he'll spend a few weeks with us before term starts again.'

'Oh good. He's enjoying Cambridge then, is he?'

'Seems to be. Mind, he only phones occasionally now, not like at first when he rang every week.'

'Well, that's youngsters for you, isn't it? I suppose it means that he's happy, though, otherwise you'd hear all about it! It's like my youngest boy—Jimmy—not that he's at university, of course—not got the brains for it—but the only time I hear from him is if he wants something. Up in Yorkshire he is, working with sheep. Poor blessed sheep, that's all I can say.'

Caroline could see a diatribe brewing on the subject of young Jimmy, so she swiftly drank

8

her coffee and made for the door.

'Well, I'll have to leave you to it if you don't mind, Mrs. Curran,' she said, grabbing her car keys, 'and get over to my mother's.'

'Right. I'll do the bathroom now then, and I'll clean the windows upstairs.'

*   *   *

It was strange really, Caroline pondered, as she drove the six or so miles to her mother's house. Mrs. Curran actually seemed to enjoy cleaning. There was a glint of true enthusiasm in her eyes as she set about her work. Caroline envied that zeal. She could think of nothing in her own life that induced eagerness or fervour in her being. It was not that she was unhappy, exactly, but she felt permanently subdued— even harnessed. She felt no passion in her heart or mind about anything. Even her lovemaking with Clive had somehow become more about her need for reassurance than any excitement born from their relationship.

She could remember neither the last time she had laughed from true pleasure, nor the last time she had cried from real sorrow. Her emotions appeared to have been nullified. Her life felt bland.

CHAPTER TWO

That evening, Caroline watched Clive as he prepared to go to his squash club. The anticipation of an hour or two spent in violent sporting exercise, followed by a couple of drinks with his friends, usually generated an affability in her husband which was not always evident, so Caroline decided to take advantage of his mood.

'I went over to Mum's today,' she began tentatively.

'Good.'

'She seems to have got over her fall now—just a nasty bruise left on her arm.'

'Good.' Clive was pre-occupied with the arrangement of new laces in his trainers.

'I don't think she should be on her own any longer, Clive.'

'How do you mean?'

'She'll be seventy-three next birthday, and I don't think she should live on her own for much longer.'

'She seems quite happy whenever I see her.'

'That isn't the point, Clive. You know Mum—she wouldn't complain, would she? That fall has made her nervous. I know it has. And I worry about her in that house with those steep stairs and everything.'

'So you think she should sell the house and

go into a home, do you?'

Clive was suddenly very attentive.

'No!'

'What then?' he asked apprehensively.

'I want her to sell up and come and live with us.' Caroline stared squarely at her husband, as his handsome face grew agitated.

'No way!' he declared, hoping to eliminate all thoughts of any argument on the subject, but failing.

'Clive . . .'

'It never works, Caro!'

'Not if the mother is an interfering old misery, I agree, but you know Mum isn't like that. She's so easy to get on with.'

'People change when you live with them, and anyway, I don't want your mother to live here.'

'Supposing one of YOUR parents was still alive, though. That would be different, wouldn't it?'

'No, it certainly would not be different, but as the question can't possibly arise, I see no point in discussing it!' Clive's movements were becoming exaggerated, and his voice was strong and harsh.

Caroline thought how extremely pompous her husband sounded.

'If you'll just calm down, Clive, I'll tell you what I thought of doing,' she reasoned.

'What?'

He stopped all activity and stared at her

11

through narrowed eyes.

'I thought we could build a granny-flat on the side of the house—an extension. There's plenty of space. Then mum could have her own rooms and I'd be able to pop in and see her whenever I wanted to, but she wouldn't interfere in our lives at all—we'd still have our privacy.'

'No, Caro, it wouldn't work.'

'Mum would help pay for the building, if that's what you're worried about. She'd get quite a bit for her house.'

'And what about the swimming pool?'

'Oh, Clive! That seems like a dreadful extravagance!'

'I don't see it like that. The piece of ground you're talking about will be ideal for the pool and that's the only thing that's going to be built there!'

'And what about mum?'

'If you really think she can't be left alone, there are some lovely places for old people now—really comfortable. There's that one over Tidbury way . . . er . . . Greenacres, or something corny like that. It's a beautiful old house. She'd have lots of company of her own age and people to look after her too.' Clive paused. 'You haven't told her she can come here, have you?' he asked curtly yet suspiciously.

'No, of course I haven't.'

'Thank God for that!'

'Clive . . . I really want mum to come and live with us. It would be the best thing for her. Please . . . think it over.' As she spoke, Caroline rebuked herself. She was pleading and she should not be. Why did she not assert herself?

'There's nothing to think about,' Clive answered, as he zipped up his sports bag in adamant manner. 'I'll get some estimates for the swimming pool next week. I've been meaning to get it started.' He kissed Caroline on the forehead. 'Really, Caro, it would never work out,' he said quietly. 'I'll see you later.'

'Caro,' she uttered, mimicking her husband's voice. 'Why can't he call me Caroline? That's my name. Too common, I suppose! You're a selfish bastard, Clive Marshall!' she called out, knowing he could no longer hear her, and gaining little satisfaction from such a futile gesture.

*   *   *

Caroline sat alone and in silence. Voiceless figures moved around on the television screen, looking ridiculous in their enforced muteness.

What would she do about her mother now? Perhaps Clive was right. Maybe it would be a mistake to have her come to live with them. Caroline wondered if it was she who was being selfish. Then it struck her just how one-sided it all was. If she could see Clive now, he would

13

be thoroughly enjoying himself—charming and gregarious as usual. He would not be doubting his motives on the question of his mother-in-law. He would not wonder whether his negative answer to Caroline's plea had been a selfish one. Oh, for that kind of confidence in one's own decisions!

Caroline had always tried to see both sides of an argument, but she was beginning to doubt the validity of this exercise. All she appeared to derive from it was an agonizing indecisiveness. Clive had often said that she was a ditherer. Once again, he was right!

How could he be so certain about everything, though? He made decisions—like the one about the swimming pool—and she went along with them. Was she a fool? No. So was it subservience then or intimidation that made her acquiesce? Surely neither should be present in a good relationship.

Money—that was part of the answer. Caroline had not worked since Adam's birth, so Clive had always been the only wage earner in their marriage. He had done very well and now, as the manager of the largest branch of Woolford's bank in the area, he savoured to the full the rewards of his position. It was probably only natural, because he was in authority when doing his job, that he should automatically assume the dominant role in other areas of his life, including at home. If she had been a career woman things might have been different. Caroline knew, though, that she could not change things—it had been as it was for far too long. A little realization, on Clive's part, that she was a woman with views and opinions, which were at least worth considering, would be welcome, however. He seemed to take very little notice of anything she said, but then, she rarely had anything of interest to say.

Caroline rested her head back on the sumptuous sofa and drifted into that pleasing yet indefinable state which comes between consciousness and sleep.

She was woken by the telephone. It was her mother.

'Oh, hello, Mum. I was going to ring you later.'

'I wondered if you were all right, dear,' her mother said cautiously. 'I thought you looked a bit peaky this morning—under the weather. Are you feeling all right?'

'Yes, I'm very well . . . really . . . I'm fine!'

'Good, that's all I wanted to know. You would tell me if anything was worrying you, wouldn't you, Caroline?'

'Yes, I would, Mum. Everything's all right. I promise.'

Caroline sat down again and turned up the volume on the television in an attempt to lose herself in the repeat of an American soap opera which was just starting. However, the programme proved less soporific than she had hoped. She found herself staring at the faces of these supposedly well-dressed women who regularly appear on the small screen. Whether their hair was bleached blonde or dyed raven black, they were clone-like in their masks. The eyes were accentuated and heavily shadowed, the cheeks blushed unnaturally up to the temples, and the lips were vivid and pouting. These managed and manoeuvred faces were totally devoid of true beauty and all individuality.

Caroline felt that she was being brainwashed. This was the way she should look. These were the women she should emulate, these ghastly, painted clowns!

'The face of the 21st Century,' she whispered. 'Women who are too afraid of rejection to refuse to conform.' She turned off the television and went to bed. She had no wish to see Clive again that night.

*   *   *

Caroline woke very early next morning. The June sun was drenching the house in a brightness she could not ignore. She had a shower but, in a stand of solitary rebelliousness, refused to weigh herself. Breakfast alone was surprisingly pleasant and, when she had finished, Caroline went out onto the patio to enjoy the freshness of the morning. She looked around the garden.

'All this, and now a swimming pool!' she muttered sarcastically to the stone fish.

The altercation of the previous evening was not mentioned when Clive came down for breakfast. In fact, conversation was decidedly sparse and Caroline felt a sense of relief when her husband left for work.

CHAPTER THREE

'Just a shampoo and blow dry today, isn't it, Mrs. Marshall?' June asked, as she combed Caroline's dripping hair into the nape of her neck.

'Yes, June.' Caroline scrutinized her hair in the rose tinted mirror. 'I don't think it needs a trim this week.'

The skilled hands of the hairdresser began to bring about the usual transformation. Caroline had frequented Maison June on the smart parade of shops near her home for some years now. June was more of a friend than one who merely gives a service, and Caroline looked forward to her weekly visit to the unisex salon.

Several girls and two young men worked for June. She had owned the business since it first opened and lived in the flat above. Caroline thought that June must be in her early thirties by now. She was tall and very slim. Her dark brown hair hung straight and shining around her shoulders and her grey eyes were always wide, enhancing her otherwise ordinary face. Caroline liked to watch June as she moved efficiently around her salon—the complete businesswoman.

'How's your mother, Mrs. Marshall? Has she got over her fall?' June asked, wishing to make her client feel as important as possible by showing that she remembered their last conversation.

'Yes, she's much better now, thanks.'

'Good. What about your son? He'll be home soon, won't he?'

'Yes, for a day or two, then he's off to France with some friends for a camping trip.'

'How lovely! I wish I'd been clever enough to go to university.'

'Mm . . . me, too.'

'They have such a terrific social life, don't they? Is your husband very brainy?'

'I suppose he is, yes.'

'I saw him last night.'

'He didn't have a haircut yesterday, did he?'

'No, no, he was just getting into his car—in Poplar Close—quite late it was.'

'I expect he took someone home after squash club and popped in for a coffee or something.'

'He's very good looking, isn't he?' June said.

Caroline could not make up her mind whether the hairdresser looked coy or envious

18

as she waited for an answer.

'Yes, he's not bad, is he?'

'Every time he comes in for a haircut the girls all argue about who's going to take his money, but don't tell him I said so, will you?'

'No, I won't.' Caroline replied, smiling with the kind of satisfaction that comes when you have something others covet.

*   *   *

Caroline had left her car at home. The weather was warm and sunny, and she enjoyed walking to the shops. On her way back, with her clean, styled hair allowing a little extra confidence to add spring to her step, Caroline stared in the pet shop window at a litter of puppies. They were plump and soft and golden, and she watched with delight as they rolled and tussled together in play. How she longed to buy one. She had always had a dog as a child and she still missed the companionship. Clive did not like animals in the house, however, he claimed that they were dirty. And now, with his brand new garden, Caroline could well imagine his reaction to a puppy. With a silent and wistful sigh, she walked on.

*   *   *

Clive was on her mind. She thought again of

19

June's words:

'He's very good looking, isn't he?' . . .

'. . . the girls all argue about who's going to take his money . . .'

'. . . Poplar Close . . . Poplar Close . . .'

Caroline could never quite admit to herself that she did not entirely trust her husband. She felt a dreadful guilt surge through her whenever she ventured to think logically on the subject. It was not that she had ever found him to be unfaithful, more that she had never looked for proof of an affair for fear of what she might discover.

Once, when Adam was only small, she had been fairly certain that there was someone else. Clive had seemed openly bored with her and had spent a great deal of time away from home. Adam took so much of her time and energy at this stage of their marriage that Caroline felt she had neglected Clive, and was unsure, at first, how to deal with the situation. If she had confronted him and found that there was another woman, he might have left her and gone to his new love. She tried, therefore, to be a model wife and give him no cause to be jealous. She had read somewhere that jealousy was a common experience among new fathers.

Eventually, Clive had returned to normal. Caroline knew that whoever or whatever had distanced him from her was gone. She never asked about it. She knew that her marriage had almost ended, though, and that dread of losing her husband and home had never left her.

Why, she wondered, could she not be like other wives? She did not want to know if her husband made love to other women. Caroline wished that she could be strong. Most women would have found out the truth and, if there had been an affair, would either have divorced him or kept a tight rein on him to make sure he never strayed again. She had done nothing. Those women, though, those women full of tough independence all too often ended up as one parent families living in a one room flat and having a nervous breakdown. Caroline had opted for security—for a home and family which were ostensibly happy and which gave relatives and friends no reason to gossip. Perhaps she was wrong to cocoon herself in deliberate ignorance, but she was not the type to struggle on alone against adversity. At least she knew her shortcomings and limitations.

Even now, though she was unsure about Clive's fidelity and in contention with him about her mother, she would not stand up and fight for what she thought was right. The consequences, if she did, might be too devastating to contemplate.

Caroline did not really blame Clive for behaving as he did but she was beginning to despise herself for her weakness and complacency. It was as though she were clinging to her battered self-respect by deceiving herself about anything which might threaten her security . . . her tedious, material security.

*   *   *

That afternoon, after basting herself in suntan lotion, Caroline lay on a sun bed in the garden. She was woken from a dream about something wonderful, which she could not recall, by Peggy, her best friend and next-door neighbour.

'You stay there, Caroline, I'll put the kettle on!' Peggy called, letting herself into the Marshalls' kitchen.

Caroline did not argue. She loved Peggy's lively company and envied her enthusiastic outlook on life.

'Lovely,' she murmured, rousing herself from her drowsy mood.

'Here you are . . . tea for two!' her friend announced, after a few minutes, as she put the tray on the ornate, plastic table.

'Thanks, Peggy.'

The two women sipped their piping hot tea.

'How are things, Caroline? Everyone all right?'

'Fine, Peggy. What about your lot?'

'The twins have gone on an outing today to London. God help the teacher! Steven's at work as usual. There's nothing very exciting happening.'

Caroline was not listening. She was trying to work out why she always said that everything was fine when she frequently felt that her life was . . . what? . . . not disintegrating . . . not in tatters . . . but . . . what? There was no crisis, no terrible trauma, but everything was no longer fine—of that Caroline was certain. So why could she not tell her best friend?

'Do you like this garden, Peggy? Please be honest,' Caroline insisted.

'Yes, it's beautiful. Why? Don't you like it?'

'I hate it!'

'But it must have cost the earth. They took a long time to do it, didn't they? What's wrong with it?'

'It's symbolic. This garden is a symbol of Clive's aspirations.'

'There's nothing wrong with wanting a lovely garden,' Peggy argued, totally bemused by her friend's words.

'But it isn't lovely! And that isn't what Clive wanted anyway. He didn't want a beautiful garden—he wanted a garden that he had bought!'

'You've lost me, Caroline.'

'We're going to have a swimming pool at the side of the house . . . over there.'

'Lucky thing!' Peggy's blue eyes widened with envy.

'You think so?'

'Well, yes . . . don't you want a pool?'

23

'No—I wanted my mother.'

'How do you mean?'

Caroline finished her tea.

'No, you're quite right, Peggy,' she said, as though waking from a trance. 'I'm very lucky.'

Peggy lay back in a garden chair. Her naturally fair hair was pulled tightly into a pony-tail and her pretty face was slightly pink from the sun so that she seemed to be permanently blushing.

She wore a tee shirt which was a little too tight and which emphasized a roll of soft fat around her waist. Her thighs bulged beneath her shorts and a second chin was developing quite rapidly under her jaw line. Peggy was plump but she didn't care.

How wonderful, Caroline thought. How absolutely wonderful not to care!

But Steven was not worried about Peggy's size either. He adored his wife and his two sons and made no secret of the fact.

Peggy and Steven laughed a lot. Caroline envied her best friend.

'Do you feel all right, love?' Peggy asked, showing real concern. 'You seem a bit preoccupied. Have you and Clive had a row?'

'No. I'm fine.' Caroline smiled broadly. 'Really . . . I'm fine.'

CHAPTER FOUR

During the following week, several builders arrived. They paced around on the plot of land at the side of the house, measuring and scribbling down figures, each one leaving with the promise that a highly competitive estimate would soon be in the post.

The subject of the swimming pool was not mentioned in the Marshalls' house.

Caroline visited her mother every other day and the old lady's cheerfulness seemed only to intensify the guilt that Caroline felt every time she left her alone. Why did she not have the courage of her convictions? Caroline agonized over this question until she realized that, to have convictions, you must be certain that your view is the right one. The luxury of such confidence in one's own judgement had always eluded her.

*   *   *

Adam's imminent arrival gave Caroline something else to think about. For this happy anticipation she was grateful.

She and her son had always been close. Before Adam's departure for Cambridge, the two of them had spent a great deal of time talking together and enjoying each other's company. Caroline had been happy to listen to Adam's youthful and often revolutionary views on such issues as politics, the third world and even mundane matters such as his homework. She had frequently found herself out of her depth intellectually. Her pride in her son's obvious brilliance, however, had made her content to listen and simply savour his presence. With Clive's evenings and weekends being taken up largely by squash and golf, she and Adam had had special times—just for the two of them.

Caroline missed Adam terribly.

The day before he was due to arrive, the house was filled with the rich aroma of cooking, as his favourite cakes and savouries were prepared for his homecoming. Mrs. Curran busied herself in Adam's room, making sure that all was in order, though she knew from past experience that the tidiness would be only short-lived.

Just after Mrs. Curran had left, Peggy tapped on the back door and opened it slowly.

'Are you on your own now, Caroline?' she asked. 'I waited until your cleaner had gone.'

'Yes, come in, Peggy!' Caroline was alarmed by her friend's anxious expression. 'Is everything all right?'

'Not really, Caroline, no.'

'Sit down and I'll make us a cuppa. What's wrong? Are the boys in trouble at school again?'

'No. Oh, Caroline . . . I've found a lump . . . in here.' Peggy pointed to her left breast and, as she did so, tears flowed freely down her face.

'Don't worry, Peggy—it's probably nothing,' Caroline said reassuringly, as she gave her friend's hand a sympathetic squeeze. She was trying desperately to hide the chilling shock that Peggy's words had caused deep inside her. 'You're going straight to the doctor, aren't you?'

'I'm frightened!'

'Yes, I can understand that, Peggy.' Caroline wanted so much to say the right thing. 'These lumps are usually nothing to worry about but you must make sure. Shall I phone and make you an appointment? You must go, dear.' Caroline placed a cup of tea on the table in front of her friend, before telephoning the doctor. 'Three-thirty this afternoon, Peggy— I'll come with you.'

'What about Steven and the twins?'

'Leave them a note saying that you've had to pop out.'

'No, I don't mean that. I mean supposing . . . supposing it IS the worst . . . and I'm going to die!' Despite Peggy's determined efforts, fresh tears found their escape from the corners of her eyes.

'Oh, Peggy, don't talk like that! It's probably nothing and even if it is a dodgy lump, they'll soon remove it. The worst you'll have is a few

27

days in hospital—that's if it comes to that—which it probably won't.'

'I suppose I'm panicking, aren't I?' Peggy's face was tortured. Caroline had never seen her so distressed. Her eyes were red and swollen from crying and terror dominated her usually cheerful countenance. Her frightened eyes searched for reassurance within Caroline's.

'Just a bit, but it's understandable. I'm sure most women would be the same. You'll feel better when you've seen the doctor.'

The day passed slowly. It seemed as if half past three would never come. Peggy spent the time with Caroline; she did not want to be alone. They talked about everything from the twins' school reports to the best recipe for a chocolate sponge cake . . . but not once did they mention cancer.

*   *   *

As she sat in the waiting room, longing fretfully for Peggy's emergence from the doctor's surgery, Caroline's eyes scanned the posters on the wall. They were all there: The Samaritans, Alcoholics Anonymous, Phobic Societies, Aids Helplines, Drugs Helplines, and so on—and so on. She pondered on the many and various problems and tragedies, which so many people have to bear. She felt humbled and very, very fortunate. She felt safe.

Peggy looked quite composed as she came out of the doctor's office.

'He wouldn't commit himself,' she whispered, 'but he told me not to worry. I've got to go to the hospital on Friday to see a specialist . . . it's a precaution they always take, apparently.'

'Yes, well it's best to be certain, isn't it? Even if it's only to put your mind at rest.'

'Mm. I feel a bit better now. He made it sound so common—having a lump—it suddenly doesn't feel so dreadful. This morning I felt like I was the only person it had ever happened to.'

'I expect you did, but doctors are dealing with it every day. Just go for this check-up on Friday, and that'll be an end to it—I'll bet you.'

'I do hope so.'

'Come on. Let's get you home.'

As they arrived outside the Marshall's house, Peggy looked at her watch.

'That's good,' she whispered, as though someone might overhear. 'No-one's home yet—I haven't been missed.' She turned to Caroline. 'Don't tell anyone about this, will you?' she pleaded.

'No, of course I won't. But don't you think you should tell Steven?'

'I'll wait and see what happens on Friday. There's no point in worrying him if there's nothing really wrong.'

'Well, if you're sure . . .'

29

'Yes. I am. I don't want them all feeling sorry for me. You won't mention it to Clive, will you?'

'No, Peggy—I promise.'

*   *   *

Caroline was up early the following morning. Though her mind settled occasionally on Adam's return, she found her joy overshadowed by thoughts of Peggy. She tried to imagine how her friend must feel . . . how she would feel.

At eleven o'clock, Caroline stood on the platform of the local railway station, awaiting Adam's train from Cambridge. It was on time, and as he stepped down to greet her—tall and handsome and smiling—she thought only of her joy at seeing him.

'Hello, mum.'

They embraced. She wanted to hold him and hold him, tighter and tighter, but she knew that he would feel embarrassed.

'Adam! It's so lovely to see you!' she enthused, wishing that she could find words which might show him how deep her joy really was, but failing in her quest.

*   *   *

Once at home, Caroline asked Adam about his course but he seemed reluctant to discuss it.

She supposed he was too excited about his trip to France, and hoped that he would elucidate more about his progress at Cambridge when his camping trip was behind him. She knew better than to pursue the subject when he clearly wished to forget all about university for a while.

That afternoon, Caroline took Adam to visit his grandmother. The old lady's pride in her only grandchild was obvious and Adam basked in the attention of these two adoring women.

'Gran looks a lot older,' he remarked as they drove home. 'Has she been ill?'

'No. She had a bad fall a couple of weeks ago which shook her up—does she look too bad, do you think?'

'Oh no—no, of course not. Don't forget I haven't seen her for a while.'

'I hope she's all right, Adam. I do worry about her.'

*   *   *

That evening, Clive and Adam talked while Caroline prepared a special meal. Everything seemed warm and comfortable and secure. Caroline wished that she could always feel like this, though if she had said that she wanted nothing else from life, it would have been a lie.

The two days that Adam spent at home were full for Caroline. She had little time to see Peggy alone, though she phoned her on her mobile whilst preparing meals and sifting through the laundry. Then, on the Friday of Peggy's hospital appointment, after she had waved Adam off, Caroline went straight to her friend's house.

'The specialist said that I've got to have the lump removed,' Peggy explained, tears welling pitifully in her eyes.

'I expect it's just a precaution,' Caroline said gently. 'Lots of people have it done. In a couple of weeks you'll be back to normal and it'll all seem like a bad dream.'

'I hope so. I've got to tell Steven when he gets home.'

'I think you'll feel better once you've told him. It does you no good to keep worries to yourself.'

'No—you're right, of course.'

Peggy began to sob. Caroline felt utterly helpless.

*   *   *

The following week, Peggy was admitted to hospital for her operation. She put on a brave face but Caroline could sense the fear, which had enveloped her best friend. She too, felt frightened.

CHAPTER FIVE

Steven was lost in sorrow without Peggy. Caroline made sure that he and the twins were fed and that their home was clean and reasonably tidy. She was relieved to be of some practical help, to feel useful. Although she could do nothing to aid Peggy's physical recovery, at least she could put her friend's mind at rest about the welfare of her family.

Cleaning Peggy's house brought with it no pressures like those Caroline remembered in her own house, in the days before Mrs. Curran had arrived like the seventh cavalry. She knew that Steven would not be critical about the standard of cleanliness as Clive had been. Peggy and Steven's home felt much more welcoming than her own show house. It reflected their easy-going way of life. The twins' muddy football boots always seemed to be on the kitchen floor, no matter how often she put them away. Computer games, books and magazines cluttered the lounge, whilst the boys' bedrooms were chaotic—it was wonderful!

*   *   *

The day after the operation, Steven came in from visiting Peggy while Caroline was still clearing up the twins' tea things.

'How is she, Steven?' she asked nervously.

'It was worse than they thought,' he replied despondently, slumping down in a chair and resting his head wearily in his hands. 'They've had to remove the breast.'

Caroline's throat seemed to close. She did not want to cry; she wanted to be strong for Steven. The effort of choking back her emotions, though, caused a tightness in her chest which became unbearable.

'I'm so sorry,' she muttered in a small, strained voice, as the tears fought the tension that held them back.

'She's coping very well,' he went on. 'Knowing Peg, though, she wants to protect me—make me think that she's not too worried about it all.'

Caroline's composure could be held intact no longer.

'Oh, Steven! I'm so sorry . . . I . . .' Seeing Caroline in tears caused, or perhaps allowed, Steven to break down also. They held each other and cried unashamedly—Steven for his wife and Caroline for her best friend.

The tears brought a little relief.

*   *   *

Clive had a squash tournament that evening and went straight from the bank to the club. Caroline sat alone in her lounge, thinking of

34

Peggy. She longed for company—young, light-hearted company. If only Adam hadn't gone to France.

Suddenly, as she tried, in vain, to interest herself in a fashionable women's magazine, deep inside her Caroline felt real panic. Her heart beat fast and her breath came in short, shallow gasps. It seemed that her head would burst. She was terrified and she could no longer sit there, alone and frightened.

Before she had time to think, she found herself in the garden. The cool evening air seemed to ease her breathing and the darkness hid the stark realities of life from her eyes. Caroline kicked off her slippers and walked on the fresh, moist lawn. The sound of the fountain intruded on the otherwise silent evening and, as she held her hands under the cascading crystals of cold water, a shiver ran through her tense body. She put her wet hands on her face and permitted herself to cry again. It was as though she were alone in the universe. She could imagine no security, no safety, anywhere. Caroline hung in a huge, black void and now the chilling water was the only sensation she could feel.

The fear, which had previously consumed her, had evaporated and been replaced by an icy numbness.

*   *   *

A car door slammed. Caroline did not know how long she had been standing there, shivering in the garden. She searched in the blackness for her slippers. Clive was home—thank God! She hurried into the house.

'David was bloody useless tonight!' he said crossly, as he entered the kitchen where Caroline stood, relieved to hear about something as unimportant and familiar as squash.

'David?' she whispered, still shaky from her ghastly experience.

'Yes—David Hines. I don't know what on earth was wrong with him. He let the whole team down!'

'Did he? Er . . . Peggy had her breast removed, Clive,' Caroline said, needing to share her unhappiness. Her words came quickly and strongly.

'Oh dear—it was cancer then—poor old Peggy.' Clive poured himself a drink.

'Yes, isn't it awful?'

'Mm. Still, that's the way it goes. The luck of the draw, I suppose.'

'But . . .'

'Look, Caro, it's no good getting yourself into a state—I can see by your face that you have been. Cancer is a terrible thing, I know, but some people get it and there's nothing you can do about that. It's a fact of life—you have to accept it.'

'I know all that, Clive. But Peggy's my best

friend!' Caroline pleaded.

'She'll be all right. They can do wonders now.' Though Clive was clearly attempting to reassure his wife, an agitation in his manner made her feel like the definitive hysterical woman.

'Yes, but I can't help feeling frightened for her.'

'You'll make yourself ill if you go on like that, Caro. Come on—pull yourself together now. I'll get you a scotch.'

Caroline knew that Clive's unemotional reaction to Peggy's illness was, in fact, the most sensible way to deal with such a crisis. Yet common sense deserted her when she thought of her lively and contented friend suddenly engulfed by such a nightmare.

That night, Caroline needed to be held by another human being. She wanted to feel that she was not alone—not isolated—not frightened.

Clive made love to her. He was passionate . . . as always.

For Caroline, it was like coming home after being away for too long. She felt reassured, wanted, needed.

'Clive,' she said softly, as they lay in the serene darkness, 'if I had to have an operation like Peggy . . . would you . . . would you still want me . . . physically, I mean?'

'There's nothing wrong with you, is there?' he asked, the gentle mood of the moment being instantly destroyed by the sharpness of his tone.

'No . . . oh, no . . . I just wondered . . . if ever there was anything . . .'

'Let's not worry about what might never happen, Caro.' Clive responded impatiently.

'I want to know, Clive. It's important to me. Would you still want to make love to me?'

'Yes, of course. Now go to sleep!'

'You're just saying that, aren't you? You hate scars—you hate any kind of imperfection, don't you? If a piece of furniture gets the slightest scratch on it, it has to go—it can't be repaired, no, that just isn't good enough, you don't want it in the house any more.'

'Well, yes . . . I suppose you're right about that,' Clive agreed grudgingly. 'I've told you before, though, we didn't have much of a home when I was a kid, what with mum dying when I was so young and dad unable to afford much in the way of luxuries on his wages. It wasn't his fault, poor old chap. He worked like hell all his life and finished up with lungs full of coal dust. It was so bloody unfair!' Clive calmed himself. 'Anyway,' he went on, 'I promised myself at a very young age that, in my life, everything would be as perfect as I could make it.'

'It isn't only furniture though, is it, Clive? What would happen if I had to have the operation Peggy's just had?'

'I don't know. For God's sake, Caro! Leave

it, will you? You're talking about something that won't happen!'

'It could do . . .' Caroline spoke quietly, but Clive was becoming louder in his tired anger.

'All right, I'd find it repulsive! There! Is that what you wanted me to say?'

'It's the truth, isn't it?'

Clive turned his back to his wife and declined to answer.

'It isn't your fault, Clive. I don't blame you,' Caroline whispered. 'I just wanted to know.'

*   *   *

The following morning a letter arrived from Adam, which lifted Caroline's spirits somewhat. He and his friends were apparently enjoying the easy life in the sunshine, and drinking far too much wine around the barbecue in the evenings.

'Oh to be young again!' Caroline whispered to herself.

She mused, for a moment, on her own youth and decided that, if she could live her teenage years again, she would have far more fun than she had done first time around. Her father had been very protective towards his only daughter and, though this protection had been a manifestation of his love for her, it had proved stifling. Life, to Caroline's father, had always been a serious and potentially dangerous business. He had seen every party she wished to attend as a prospective brawl or, even worse, an orgy and every young man as a seducer.

Caroline knew that some of her father's anxieties had influenced her greatly. His idea of home was a place to be safe, away from the more damaging and evil aspects of life—an idyllic haven in a wicked world. Her version was diluted but her need for a home and family was real. The thought of living alone still frightened her.

*   *   *

A visit to Peggy, that afternoon, proved to be a far more uncomfortable experience than Caroline had expected.

The two women had known each other for more than fifteen years and yet, as they sat there, it was as though they were strangers in the compartment of a train, who were trying to alleviate the tedium of a long journey by indulging in a little trite conversation.

At last, after several minutes of this false and wearing situation had caused a knot to form in Caroline's stomach, Peggy spoke to her as an old friend once more, with trust and in confidence.

'I can't bear to look at myself, Caroline,' she whispered. 'It's a big scar, I can feel that much ... but I don't want to see it.'

'You'll feel differently soon, Peggy. It's early

days yet. It's been a shock . . . you're bound to feel apprehensive.'

'I feel mutilated!'

'Don't say that, dear! Can't they do a reconstruction job? That's what they call it, isn't it?'

'I don't relish the idea of more surgery,' Peggy said thoughtfully, 'and anyway, it wouldn't be me, would it? I'd be partly plastic, like having a false arm or leg, only worse.'

'Why worse?'

'Because . . . because it's my breast . . . my femininity . . . do you understand?'

'Yes. I do.'

Caroline thought back to the previous night. Her comprehension of her friend's distress was far greater than Peggy could ever have realized.

'It's a strange phenomenon, you know, Caroline—to be literally frightened to look in the mirror—or to look down at your own body. I tried to imagine earlier what I must look like now—to prepare myself—but I felt sick, so I stopped.'

'Give yourself time, Peggy.'

'The trouble is, I don't think that I'll be able to come to terms with what has happened until I do face myself honestly and admit to myself that I am no longer a whole woman. There's no peace of mind all the time we refuse to face the truth, is there?'

Caroline left the hospital with much on her mind, in particular . . . the truth.

Yes, Peggy was right. The best way to deal with your problems is to face them. Caroline decided that she would accompany Clive to the golf club that evening.

She too would pursue the truth

CHAPTER SIX

Whilst Clive finished his dinner that evening, Caroline disappeared upstairs to return ten minutes later in a new, and very stylish, cream dress, which complimented her suntan beautifully. She wore large pearl earrings and a necklace to match. Her hair and make-up were perfect.

'I thought I'd come and have a drink with you at the golf club tonight,' she announced, watching closely for Clive's reaction.

'What? Oh—right,' he replied, unable to conceal his surprise, not only at Caroline's revelation that she was about to accompany him, but also that she had made the decision unaided, and declared her intentions with an uncharacteristic assertiveness. 'I thought you hated all the people at the golf club,' he went on.

'Yes, I do. But I hate being alone even more—just at the moment, anyway.'

'I see . . . well, I'll shower and be down in fifteen minutes. Then you can come and hate my friends all over again.'

Caroline resolved that she would try to be positive about the people she met that evening. She would look for their goodness and ignore the pretentiousness that she had found so annoying on her previous visits to the club. After all, it must surely be a juvenile generalization to label all the members as arrogant social climbers who have an in-built belief that they are superior beings.

Yes, she must be more tolerant.

*   *   *

As they settled at a table near the bar, David Hines, the assistant manager at Clive's bank, joined the Marshalls.

'Well, Caroline! We don't often have the pleasure of your company at the nineteenth hole!' he said, as he kissed her cheek. 'I'd have brought Jenny along if I'd known and made a foursome.'

'How is Jenny?' Caroline asked.

'Oh, not so bad. Still tired out and still teaching.'

'It's time you two came to dinner again,' suggested Clive. 'Get Jenny to give Caro a call and make a date.'

43

'You've forgiven me for my diabolical performance last night then, Clive?' David joked.

'Oh, yes, the squash,' Caroline put in, as the horror of the previous evening passed fleetingly but painfully across her mind. She drew herself back to the present, not allowing the ghastly fear she had known to remain for more than a moment in her thoughts.

David was not a pleasant young man, Caroline pondered, as she watched him and Clive chatting about the defeated squash team and the doubtful merits of the victors. He wanted to be like Clive—that was obvious. He looked at his boss with what amounted to hero-worship in his eyes. Caroline felt a kind of pity for David. He certainly did not have Clive's good looks, and it seemed to her that he would always be a runner-up in life—a man who was a deputy, a man who let the squash team down—sad, really. David's ambition to be like Clive is what caused Caroline to dislike him. She knew that if he should ever succeed in managing a branch somewhere, he would be Clive Mk II—another man steeped in his own self-importance and sitting smugly on an inflated ego. No, Caroline did not like David Hines. He was an embryo Clive, but without her love.

Jenny, his wife, was the career woman epitomized. She was the deputy head of a local primary school, awaiting, rather impatiently, her own promotion to headmistress and her husband's to bank manager. The Hines had one daughter of about ten years old. Caroline marvelled at the ease in which Jenny seemed to divide her time between her demanding job and her family, depriving neither of the attention with they obviously commanded.

She would ask Jenny and David to dinner soon. Jenny was pleasant enough company and Caroline was determined to avoid too many lonely evenings in the future. She needed people at the moment. More than she had ever done before.

Caroline stared around the room, which was becoming quite crowded and rather smoky. She looked at each table in turn. The faces were vaguely familiar but she could put names to none of them. Although she had been introduced to quite a few of the regulars on her previous visits, they had not seemed to be significant to her—eminently forgettable, in fact.

As she looked around at the men in their casual, but expensive, golfing attire and their wives, with eyes shadowed in blues and greens, adding a further air of falsehood to their already exaggerated but hollow smiles, Caroline realized what it was that angered her so much about these people. They all reminded her of Clive—the side of him that she loathed. Yes, she did admit to herself that she hated at least one aspect of her husband's character—that part of him which longed to impress—impress in the wrong ways—in all the superficial, unimportant ways.

Caroline watched these friends of Clive's, mesmerized. She wondered if any of their conversations were about anything of any consequence. Indeed, she wondered whether they would EVER say anything of any consequence, or if they would continue to babble inanely until they took their final breath, always preferring to talk rather than to listen.

Just as she had begun a little self-reproach at her hostile attitude towards these people, Caroline became intrigued by the conversation at her own table.

'. . . yes . . . rather pretty, she is,' David was saying, '. . . blonde . . . lives in one of those big, detached houses in Poplar Close.'

'What about her?' Clive asked in an indifferent manner.

'Her father is in computers, she was telling me—could be useful, I thought.'

'We've got enough experts of our own,' Clive replied, with a certain dominance in his tone.

'Did you say Poplar Close?' Caroline interrupted.

'Yes, he did. Why?' Clive answered, with what his wife suspected to be sheepishness.

'I was driving around that area the other day,' Caroline explained. 'There are some beautiful houses in Poplar Close, aren't there?'

'Yes. They're obviously quite well-off, Diane's family,' said David, with the innocence which only ignorance can provide in his eyes.

'Diane?' Caroline inquired, wishing to learn as much as she could about the girl she now believed was her husband's mistress.

'Mm. Diane Tully,' David obliged eagerly. 'She's a new teller at the bank. Well, she's been with us for about six weeks now, I suppose.'

'I see,' Caroline replied quietly. Clive was silent. He looked straight ahead, evidently having no wish to continue with this particular topic of conversation.

The rest of the evening was nothing less than an ordeal for Caroline.

She sat in the midst of the noisy room, hearing nothing and, through the hazy grey atmosphere, she saw only Clive's handsome face. Her emotions were so heightened that she found it impossible to think rationally.

An anger, so fierce inside her, made her clench her fists rather than allow them to physically attack her unfaithful man. She wanted to hurt him, to punch him, to claw at his skin and scar his perfect features. Yet, in the same heartbeat, she longed to hold him, to make love to him as she had never done before, to be so perfect a lover that there could be no need in him for any other woman.

Caroline ached to possess him and to prove to herself that he was hers alone . . . but she also longed for revenge. In the same mind and the same heart, she wanted so much to kill him.

'Are you all right, Caroline?' David asked, touching her arm and jolting her back to a reality as dreadful as her innermost thoughts.

'Yes . . . yes, I'm fine.'

'Clive's gone to get you another drink.'

'Has he?' Caroline picked up her handbag. 'I want to go home,' she uttered, her voice breaking deep in her throat.

Clive returned with a white wine for Caroline. She stood up.

'I'll wait for you in the car, Clive,' she said sharply. 'Good night, David.'

Clive stared in bewilderment as he watched his wife leave the clubroom.

*　　　*　　　*

They drove home in silence.

Clive's physical closeness to her made Caroline feel both sensuous and repulsed.

All the words of fury that had simmered in her mind while they had sat in the golf club had faded now that the opportunity was there to voice them. She must think. It would be stupid to blurt out all that she felt now. She needed to compose herself.

It was strange, she thought, that Clive had not questioned her about her behaviour in the club. Had he guessed that she had found him

48

out? Caroline needed to be alone—only without Clive would she be able to order her thoughts.

They went to bed as usual, except that scarcely a word passed between them.

Caroline lay still until she was sure Clive was asleep, then slid silently out of bed and put on her dressing gown. She made herself a large mug of cocoa and sat in the lounge by the dim light of a table lamp.

At this moment, she felt relief at being alone.

Could she be mistaken? That was the first question to emerge from the dire confusion of her thoughts. She had reverted to her customary doubt in her own judgement quite without noticing. It was possible that Clive had taken someone else home to Poplar Close on the night that June had seen him, or maybe another member of the squash club lived in the same road. There had been a guilt about him, though, when Diane Tully had been spoken of; Caroline was certain of that. Or was it her imagination, her suspicious eyes seeing what they expected to see?

She would say nothing yet. She would wait until she was sure. Her eyelids were heavy and the warm drink had soothed her churning insides. She closed her eyes and her mind drifted back over the day's events.

When she had left Peggy, she had been determined to face those facts in her life that she had always avoided. She wanted to be strong, to find peace of mind by being honest with herself, but now . . . now that she had faced the turmoil which her quest had brought, Caroline felt very unhappy.

If the close companion of truth was always going to be pain, then perhaps ignorance really does bring that elusive bliss. Or maybe she was simply too weak to cope with self-honesty.

The problem was that having planted deep, agonizing doubts about Clive in her own mind once again, she felt compelled this time to find out whether or not they were groundless. She prayed that they were.

Caroline hated herself.

*   *   *

The next morning she mumbled to Clive that she had woken up with a headache and would stay in bed for an extra hour to try to rid herself of it.

Yes, she thought, as she pulled the duvet up around her shoulders and closed her eyes against the morning light, Clive could get his own breakfast. Pouring out his orange juice and putting his muesli into a cereal bowl would not tax him to any great extent, after all. Caroline rebuked herself for the sarcasm, which she felt was becoming an all too prominent part of her personality.

When she came downstairs, Clive had gone,

as had her headache. She was glad that she had avoided early morning conversation with him.

*   *   *

Caroline left Mrs. Curran at work and drove to Clive's bank. Her curiosity was too acute to be ignored. She sat down in the customers' waiting area, knowing that Clive would be hidden safely away in his office.

Her troubled eyes studied each of the tellers behind the polished wood counter. Some of them she knew quite well. Her gaze came to rest. There she was—Miss Diane Tully. The small sign bearing her name allowed her no anonymity. Her blonde hair fell in loose curls around her shoulders, her full bosom being much in evidence through her flimsy blouse. Some men would, no doubt, consider her to be pretty, but to Caroline—and womankind in general—Diane Tully's face was common and showed a cheapness, which was born from her character rather than her features.

'Hello, Mrs. Marshall. Do you want your husband?' a cheery voice asked.

'Hello . . . it's Rachel, isn't it?' said Caroline to a short, dumpy young woman.

'Yes, that's right. We met at the Christmas party.'

'Of course. No, dear, I did pop in to ask Clive something, but I've changed my mind—it

51

isn't important—I'll see him later.'

'Oh, right.'

'Rachel,' Caroline began tentatively, 'you've been with this branch for some time now, haven't you?'

'Yes, nearly two years, Mrs. Marshall.'

'I thought so. You've got one or two new girls here now, though—I'm sure I don't recognize them all.'

'Oh yes, there's Sarah—she's only been here for a week, and then there's Diane—she started a couple of months ago.'

'Nice girls are they? It makes such a difference if you all get on well together, doesn't it?'

'Yes, we all get on all right. Mind, I'm not too keen on Diane. Though I suppose I shouldn't say so.'

'Really?' Caroline sounded surprised, but in truth she was not. 'She looks like the kind of girl who boasts about her boyfriends,' she whispered. 'Am I right?'

'Not boys, Mrs. Marshall—men!'

'Oh!' Caroline and Rachel giggled like schoolgirls in the playground, but for the former, the laughter was false and laborious.

Rachel felt just a little uncomfortable, yet at the same time flattered, at having this conversation with an older woman who also happened to be the boss's wife.

'Oh, yes, she likes the older man, does our Diane!' Rachel went on. 'She's always going on

52

about her love life.'

'I can imagine.' Caroline nodded, both to illustrate her understanding of Diane's type and to encourage further elucidation.

'Apparently this one she's got now buys her expensive presents—jewellery and perfume—that sort of thing. She says he's old enough to be her father, but he's supposed to be very handsome.'

'Is he now?'

'Mind you, I don't believe it all, Mrs. Marshall. I think she dreams up half her stories!'

'Probably. Trying to create an impression, I expect. Anyway, dear, I must be off. Nice to see you again.'

*   *   *

Although Caroline still had no real proof of Clive's infidelity, as she drove back home, her anger rose once more to the surface.

'Common little slut!' she muttered, her jaws tense and her lips tightened across her teeth. 'You're a swine, Clive Marshall! A bloody animal!'

She flung her car keys down on the hall table as she entered. Mrs. Curran had left.

Caroline dropped onto the sofa in the lounge, stretched out and closed her eyes.

To think that a short time ago she had felt her life to be bland. She could no longer make that claim. Her emotions were in full working order . . . functioning to the maximum.

She wished that the calm would return. She was not enjoying the storm.

CHAPTER SEVEN

As she prepared to visit her mother that afternoon, Caroline wondered what David Hines must have made of her unusual behaviour at the club the night before. He probably went home and told the efficient Jenny that Caroline Marshall was cracking up. No doubt Clive had attributed her hurried departure and prolonged silence to pre-menstrual tension; that was his usual answer when her behaviour deviated from the norm in any way. Unless, of course, he had realized that she was suspicious about him and Diane Tully . . . no . . . he would never have credited her with such perception.

Caroline deliberated on whether or not she should confide in her mother about Clive's possible infidelity. She did not want to worry the old lady but she felt that if she talked to no one about her distrust of him, she would go out of her mind.

The worst part was that no matter how hard she tried to think of other things, she kept seeing Clive and that girl together . . .

embracing . . . kissing . . . making love . . . no, not making love—having sex. There could be no love between Clive and that tart.

Caroline was in absolute torment. She would have to question him—confront him—she could not go on like this. Suppose she was wrong, though? How could she be certain? Perhaps she should follow him . . .

The doorbell rang.

*   *   *

Caroline answered the front door to find a young girl standing there, who looked like a student in her jeans and T-shirt.

'Is Adam Marshall in, please?' she asked politely.

'No, he isn't. He's in France, actually.'

'Oh.' The girl was clearly disappointed.

'Do come in, dear,' Caroline said. 'Have you come far?'

'From Cambridge,' the girl replied, following Caroline into the kitchen.

'I'm so sorry he isn't here—he's camping with friends—if only you'd telephoned first.'

'Yes, I should have done. I didn't think.'

'Would you like some tea?' Caroline asked, hoping that the girl would not be staying for too long, but feeling that a little refreshment might compensate, in some small way, for a wasted journey.

'Thanks, yes, I would.' She sat down at the

breakfast bar.

'What's your name, dear?' Caroline inquired, as she hurriedly made the drink.

'Christine—Christine Jordan.'

'Are you at college with Adam?'

'No. I live in Cambridge, though.'

'Oh, I see.' Caroline sat down with the girl, wishing she could draw her into more enlightening conversation but guessing that Christine was shy. 'Are you and Adam friends, then?' she continued.

'Yes, I work in a bookshop near his college. That's how we met.'

'Oh, that's nice. He's gone to France with four other boys—they're having a good time, according to his letter. I'm surprised he didn't tell you he was going.'

'I didn't see him at the end of term, otherwise I expect he would have done. When will he be back?'

'He didn't give us a definite date—all he said was five to six weeks. If you give me your phone number, I'll get him to ring you when he gets home. That's the best I can do, I'm afraid.'

'Six weeks!' the girl repeated. She sighed and stood up to leave.

Caroline's heart went out to this rather timid youngster. Perhaps she had a crush on Adam; she looked so forlorn.

'I'm so sorry I can't be of more help, Christine,' Caroline apologized. 'Can I give him a message at all, if he phones us?'

'You can tell him I'm expecting his baby, if you like!' announced Christine.

Caroline was astounded and silent. For a moment she sat staring in dumbfounded disbelief at the girl who had delivered this shock to her.

The girl was walking towards the front door, tea untouched.

'No! No, wait!' Caroline shouted. 'Come back! You must . . . we have to talk!' She led the girl into the lounge and, having taken a deep breath, she spoke quietly, trying to appear calm and approachable but knowing that yet another emotional bomb was about to explode in her life, scattering its debris over her already perplexed state of mind. 'Let's hear all about this, please, Christine.'

The girl sat down and Caroline saw that she was near to tears. She looked closely at Christine for the first time. Her young face was freckled and naturally pretty. Her hair was dark brown with waves that hung very long and bushy down ·her back. As she glanced tentatively at Caroline, a disarming honesty shone from her brown eyes.

'I love Adam,' said Christine, with an earnestness that left Caroline in no doubt that she spoke the truth.

'And how does he feel about you?'

'We haven't known each other all that long—four or five months, I suppose. He told me that he loved me and he was so good to me that I know he must have meant it. Then, in the last week of term, I didn't see him. He was never around when I tried to contact him. I've been so miserable. When I found I was pregnant, I thought that I should come and tell him face to face—it's his baby, too, after all.'

'Are you sure you ARE pregnant?'

'No doubt about it; I'm two months.'

'And Adam is . . .'

'Yes, Mrs. Marshall,' Christine interrupted, having anticipated Caroline's question with some indignation, 'Adam is definitely the father. He's the only boy I've ever been with.'

Caroline was at a loss. What should she do? How should she deal with this?

'We can't contact Adam,' she muttered. 'We don't know where he is. He wouldn't even take his mobile—said he wanted to be absolutely free!'

Christine pushed back her fringe. The movement appeared to be a nervous habit, but it made her look so very young.

'I'd better get back home, Mrs. Marshall. I should really be speaking to Adam about this . . . though I wish we could have discussed it before I tell my parents . . .'

'Your parents!' gasped Caroline, not having considered their existence until now. 'You mean you haven't told them?'

'No. I've been afraid to. I thought if I could tell them that Adam and I had worked everything out—our future, that is—it might help. I thought that perhaps they would accept the situation more easily.'

'Why haven't you told anyone before?'

Christine bowed her head.

'I hoped, at first, that it was a false alarm—that I wasn't pregnant. I was putting off the moment of truth, I suppose. I've only just found out for certain, so I came straight here to find Adam.'

'How do you think your parents will take the news?'

'My dad will go mad. My mum will probably be more upset than angry. It's still a frightening prospect—telling her. I'm an only child, you see, like Adam. They'll think I've let them down—I'm all they've got.'

'Do you live with your parents?'

'Yes, but I've told them I'm staying with friends for a couple of days. I thought it would take that long to talk it all through with Adam, so I brought some spare clothes in my rucksack; I was going to get a room at a B&B or a hostel or something.'

Caroline chewed her lower lip as she mulled over their conversation and tried to take in all that Christine had said.

'Well . . . why don't you stay here, Christine? Mr. Marshall and myself would like to help you, if we can. And there's always the chance that Adam might phone.'

'I don't know,' Christine answered

hesitantly. 'Now that I'm here I feel I shouldn't have come.'

'Please stay,' Caroline implored. 'I feel . . . some responsibility for you. Adam is my son. If you walk out now, I'll worry about you . . . and the baby. I'll wonder what's happening to you and how you are. I'd also like to get to know you—you obviously mean a lot to Adam.'

After a few moments thought, Christine agreed to stay for a couple of days.

'Thank you, you're very kind,' she murmured. 'I hope my mum and dad can be as reasonable as you.'

Christine seemed so frightened, so vulnerable somehow, that Caroline felt protective towards her, even though they had only just met.

Caroline showed the girl up to the spare room. While Christine was unpacking, Caroline phoned her mother and explained that she would not be able to visit that day as a friend of Adam's had arrived unexpectedly. She did not tell the old lady about the baby; that would take a special visit and lots of courage. It was not that she would be angry exactly, but her views on such matters were rather old-fashioned and she would certainly be distressed.

Caroline pondered on the stupidity of her son and Christine. How could they have been so foolish? To think of Adam fathering a child was incredible to her. He had hardly shown any interest in girls before going to Cambridge. In this day and age, when safe sex was being preached everywhere you turned, had they not even thought to use precautions? What idiots! And what would Clive say?

The only remotely positive outcome of the afternoon's events was that Caroline's mind was no longer dwelling solely on Clive and Diane Tully. She now had other matters, which demanded her fevered attention.

*   *   *

When he came home from work, Caroline took Clive to one side and told him about Christine and Adam, hoping that she could placate his predictable anger before he met the girl. Clive was angry all right, though not in the way she had expected—he was not angry with Adam.

'You should have sent her packing, Caro!' he stormed, having giving forth with some preliminary expletives. 'It probably isn't Adam's baby at all!'

'It is, Clive. She isn't a liar—you can see that she's a genuine sort of girl.'

'Well, I'd like to hear Adam's side of things before we get involved,' Clive continued.

'But we are involved!' Caroline argued. 'The girl is terrified of telling her parents, she can't find Adam . . . so we're the only ones who know. I feel sorry for her.'

'Well I don't! It takes two, you know, Caro. The days of blaming the boy are over.'

'I'm not blaming Adam alone, Clive. They both need help in a situation like this.'

'So you invited her to stay here. For God's sake, Caro!' Clive took a deep, exasperated breath. 'Look,' he went on, 'if she has an abortion, they can both get on with their lives as if nothing has happened. Adam has his degree to think about. It's no good this girl thinking he can give up his course and a good career to provide for her and the baby.'

'Oh, Clive, no! Not an abortion! I don't think so . . . that's so wrong . . . so very, very wrong. And, anyway, Christine will want to keep the child—I'm sure she will. She says she loves Adam.'

'But she isn't a student, is she?'

'No, she works in a bookshop.'

'Probably isn't from a very good family, then.'

'Clive!'

'You've got to face facts, Caro. We can't let Adam throw away the chance of a degree and a decent career because of a mistake with this girl. An abortion is the best way out.'

Where was Clive's compassion? Caroline wondered in bewilderment. He appeared to care nothing about Christine's feelings; he did not even try to understand her plight. Clive seemed so calculating. When he finally met the girl, he was civil but cold and rather harsh.

Caroline stared with contempt at her husband. The doubts, which she had about his own moral behaviour, added to her anger at his attitude now.

After a very awkward meal, during which no one felt able to broach the subject of Christine's pregnancy, Clive went out into his garden. He mowed the lawn and scoured the flowerbeds for weeds. Caroline was simply thankful that he was not in the house.

Christine had gone to bed by the time Clive came back in. He watched a programme about finance and the stock exchange on the television. Caroline thought about her unborn grandchild and about its young mother crying herself to sleep upstairs in the spare room. She took a tranquillizer.

*   *   *

Caroline felt she could talk to Christine again once Clive had left for work.

'He doesn't like me, does he—Mr. Marshall?' the girl said as they drank their mid-morning coffee. 'He thinks I'm common—I can tell.'

'Not at all, Christine! It was just a bit of a shock—that's all. Men . . . well, they don't always understand how we feel, or see things in the same way as we do, do they?'

'I don't know what to do about my mum and dad.'

'Well, you'll have to tell them, won't you? I don't see any way around that.'

'There's one way.'

'What do you mean?'

'If I had an abortion. I could tell my mum and dad that I was staying with friends and they need never know.'

'Is that what you want, Christine? To get rid of your child?'

'I don't think I've got much choice, have I? I've been lying awake all night thinking about it. Adam won't want to give up his course and keep me and the baby. I can see that now and it wouldn't be fair to ask him to. The last thing I want to be is a burden to him. As for my parents—dad's a road sweeper for the council and doesn't earn much money and mum has chronic arthritis, so I couldn't ask her to look after the baby while I go out to work.'

'The State would give you something, Christine, and I dare say Mr. Marshall would help out financially.'

'No. No, I wouldn't want that.'

'It would only be until Adam was working, then he'd keep the child, of course. Perhaps you'd be married by then, anyway.'

'I wish Adam was here! I want to know what he thinks I should do! I need to know how he feels about it all!'

'I know, dear. I understand.'

Caroline was becoming fond of this unfortunate girl. She wished so much that she could help her in some way.

The thought of Adam and Christine being in love made her feel somehow defensive towards them both. She was sorry about the baby and angered by their foolishness yet, at the same time, she wanted to look after them and help them through their present difficulties. She wanted them to have a happy ending.

The idea of abortion was abhorrent to Caroline.

CHAPTER EIGHT

After lunch, Christine relaxed in the Marshalls' garden while Caroline visited Peggy. She prayed that Adam would phone while Christine was alone, but he did not.

Peggy looked far stronger than on Caroline's previous visit. The colour was returning to her face and she seemed to have a more positive attitude towards her illness.

'I got over that business about looking at myself,' she explained to Caroline. 'The nurses left me on my own in the bathroom this morning, so I stood in front of the mirror and took off my nightie. It was strange, really. Once I had looked at myself, I couldn't stop. I stared and stared for ages; it was as though I had to become acquainted with my new body—to accept it—and I have.'

'That's great,' Caroline said softly. 'I'm so glad you're feeling better about things.'

'Goodness knows what Steven will think of me,' Peggy went on, her smile failing to hide from Caroline that she was concerned about what her husband's reaction would be.

'He'll think the same thing as he always has done!' Caroline said reassuringly.

'Yes, I suppose he will. I was mulling it over earlier . . . for heaven's sake, listen to me . . . I've thought of nothing else! But I decided this morning that it's me that Steven loves—me, the person—and the scars on the exterior shouldn't make any difference, should they? If they do turn him off me, then his feelings must always have been pretty superficial, don't you think?'

'Steven adores you, Peggy. He'll be so relieved to have you back home and well again, that he'll hardly notice your scars!'

'I'm not so sure about that, Caroline. They're fairly conspicuous, you know—I am minus one breast. But he'll soon come to terms with it, won't he? Like I've had to.'

'Of course he will. You've no worries about Steven.'

Caroline's heart ached when she thought of Clive's reaction to her questions on the subject. Indeed, she was realizing that his feelings for her must be extremely superficial. What with hypothetical flaws on her body

66

repulsing him, and his apparent attraction to the well-rounded Miss Tully—not much chance of her having any imperfections—his love for Caroline could hardly be described as deep and undying.

'Are you all right, Caroline?' Peggy asked, seeing once more that far away look, which was becoming all too much of a permanent feature on her friend's face.

'Yes, I'm all right. Just a bit worried about Adam, that's all.'

Caroline had opted to confide in Peggy about Christine's news rather than her own marital problems. To tell of Clive's suspected escapades with Diane Tully would be more of an admission of failure somehow, than to speak of Adam's misdemeanour, though she was unsure why. Perhaps it was because when problems with one's offspring cause concern, there is a kind of empathy which parents share—the child who causes no anxiety having yet to be born. Whereas, when one admits to a marital difficulty, especially one to do with sex, a deep feeling of personal failure seems to emerge from the idea that there must be something lacking in one's own sexual prowess.

Caroline could not imagine Clive ever doubting his attractiveness, nor his virility. But then, he had no reason to.

Peggy could only sympathize with Caroline about Adam and Christine's predicament, but just to talk about it, with someone other than Clive, allowed Caroline to feel some relief from her present burden of unhappiness. Peggy, too, found some escape from her own problems in discussing someone else's. Caroline was glad that her friend was looking out into the world again. These two women had a very special relationship.

*   *   *

Christine went to bed soon after dinner that evening. She wanted an early start, so she said, in order to catch the first train to Cambridge the following day, but Caroline was fairly certain that the atmosphere created by Clive's presence in the house was the main reason for Christine's hasty retirement to the spare room.

'You haven't made that poor girl feel at all welcome, Clive,' Caroline began, once they were alone.

'That's because she isn't welcome,' was the curt response.

'Don't you feel any compassion for her at all?'

'No—absolutely none.'

'Have you tried to imagine how she feels?'

'I should think she feels pretty damn stupid!' Clive's face was fierce, but quite wonderful in its ferocity.

'Why stupid?'

'Well, she should have been on the pill,

shouldn't she? If she intended to sleep around, she should have taken precautions.'

'But she isn't like that, Clive. You can see she's a decent girl. She told me that Adam is the only boy she's ever been with.'

'Maybe, maybe not. We have no way of knowing.'

'Anyway, why should Christine go on the pill just in case she meets a boy she likes a lot? Why didn't Adam take any precautions?'

'He probably took it for granted that she was on the pill—most girls are, you know.'

'You're an authority on that subject, are you, Clive?'

'I thought it was common knowledge. Come on, Caro—don't be naïve!'

'Naïve,' Caroline echoed, more to herself than her husband. 'No, I must never be that, must I?'

There was a pause while Clive poured himself a drink and Caroline pondered on how many times he had deceived her during their marriage—on just how often she had been naïve.

'Try to be a little more pleasant in the morning,' she went on. 'Christine may be our daughter-in-law soon.'

'God forbid!' Clive burst out.

'What would be so terrible about that?' Caroline asked. 'She's a very sweet girl. I've come to like her a lot. You might have done, too, if you'd given her half a chance!'

'Adam could do a lot better for himself,' Clive answered. He stared with hard, unyielding eyes at Caroline. 'He's intelligent, good-looking and he's completing his education at one of the best universities in the world! He could go where he likes, do what he likes and command a good salary in whatever he does. Do you want him to throw away a financially sound future so that he can marry this girl and keep her child for her?'

'Her name is Christine!' Caroline snapped irritably. 'And it's Adam's child, too! I know it's convenient to forget that but we must face the facts!'

'Don't you want him to have a good start, Caro?'

'Of course I do! But you only seem to consider money and the standard of living it can buy, Clive. What about old fashioned happiness? Perhaps he really loves Christine.'

'Happiness—old fashioned or otherwise—is a lot easier to come by if you're not broke! Anyway, they're only kids!' Clive stormed.

'So were we,' whispered Caroline.

Clive finished his drink and quickly poured himself another.

'The best thing she can do is to have an abortion,' he continued, with his customary firmness, 'then they won't be tied to each other, will they? It'll be better for both of them.'

'We could help them, Clive,' Caroline

suggested gently. 'If they do want to marry . . . if they are in love. Adam could continue with his course and we could have Christine and the baby to live here. They'd get money from the State to help with their keep and at least they wouldn't have to pay rent or anything. Christine could even get a job once the baby is born—I'd enjoy looking after it for her.'

'Don't be ridiculous, Caro!' Clive looked truly appalled at his wife's proposal. 'You're being over-emotional about all this. Think about what you're saying!'

'I have thought about it!'

'We don't want a baby in the house!'

'You don't, you mean!'

'And neither do you! Crying at all hours of the night, nappies everywhere—think what it would be like. Our lives wouldn't be our own! We'd have no privacy at all. First it was your mother and now this!'

'It would enable Adam to get his degree, though, wouldn't it? And it would only be for a couple of years, until he gets a job. Then they could afford somewhere of their own.'

'I'm telling you, Caro, if that girl moves in here—I move out!'

Caroline was sure that Christine must have heard them rowing. She thought of the girl's state of mind and how terribly alone she must feel.

Clive turned on the television, indicating that the subject was closed.

Caroline lay alone in bed. Having tried to read several pages of a book but finding she knew nothing of the content, she put it aside and lay staring at the ceiling.

For a while she seriously contemplated calling Clive's bluff. If she asked Christine to live with them, would he really go?

And would it be such a terrible loss if he did?

What was it that prevented her risking his leaving? She no longer trusted him. She hated his lack of compassion and his grossly materialistic way of life. For most of the time, she even felt that she was tethered to his job, his home, and his ghastly garden.

So why did she not send him away? Let him go to his Diane? Because she needed him there, with her, and because she loved him, for God's sake. She loved the awful man!

CHAPTER NINE

'It looks as if it might brighten up later,' Mrs. Curran commented, as she started to clean the kitchen floor with such vigorous and determined movements of her mop that an onlooker might have suspected that her life depended on the spotlessness of the ivory tiles.

'The weather forecast was for a bright afternoon.'

Caroline stood staring out of the kitchen window, aware of her cleaner's presence but hearing nothing of her mundane witterings.

'Do you know what I'd really like to do, Mrs. Curran?' Caroline asked wistfully.

'No . . . what?'

'I'd like to dig up that lawn and those neat, tidy flower beds, get rid of that pond—or well, or whatever it is—and that stupid fish fountain. Then, when it was all dug up, I'd like to plant hundreds and hundreds of wild flowers . . . so that I could have my very own meadow.'

The swish of Mrs. Curran's mop hesitated before coming to a stop as the cleaner was somewhat taken aback, not only by what her employer was saying, but by the fact that Caroline was talking from her heart and not indulging in the usual platitudinous conversation.

'Oh, would you?'

'Did you know that there are hardly any meadows left?' Caroline continued, fixing her eyes on the garden, dreamy and still.

'I hadn't thought about it,' the cleaner replied, leaning on her mop, 'but now that you mention it . . . there aren't many, are there? Not like when I was a girl.'

Caroline sighed.

'Just hundreds and hundreds of wild flowers. Wouldn't that be wonderful?'

Before Mrs. Curran could answer, Christine entered the kitchen with her travel-bag in hand.

*   *   *

The drive to the station was a forlorn affair. Caroline felt she had had the opportunity to help Christine, but that she had failed totally.

'Are you going to tell your parents about the baby?' she asked.

'No, I can't . . . I've thought about it a great deal but there would be such awful rows. They'd be so upset and angry and I just couldn't cope with all that—not now, not on top of everything else.'

'What will you do then?'

'I'm going to have a termination.' Christine bowed her head and her voice trembled to a murmur. 'I think it's for the best.'

'Oh, Christine . . . do be sure before . . .'

'Before I kill my child? Before I kill Adam's child?' the girl put in, as tears filled her sad eyes.

'No . . . I didn't mean that, but it's too late to be sorry afterwards. Real regret can be agony, you know.'

'If I was absolutely sure that Adam really loved me, then it would be different. But if he only thought of me and the baby as a nuisance, as a stupid mistake that had ruined his plans . . . well . . . I just couldn't bear that.'

'I'm sure that Adam cares for you very much,' Caroline said kindly.

'I don't know. I thought he did, but that last week of term when I couldn't find him . . . it's made me wonder if he was avoiding me on purpose . . .trying to let me know that he didn't want to see me any more.'

'I expect he was just busy, finishing off his college work before the holidays.'

'I'm really not sure, Mrs. Marshall. He certainly didn't try to find me, did he? If he really loved me, he would surely have wanted to say goodbye before he left for home.'

'Oh, Christine, I so wish that I could have helped you. I'll get Adam to phone you the moment he gets back.'

'I think that'll be too late. I just hope he isn't angry with me. When he arrives, please explain that I tried to ask him what he wanted me to do but that I had to make the decision without him, won't you?'

'Of course,' Caroline replied gently.

On the platform, the woman and the girl embraced fondly. As Caroline watched Christine walk to the train, it was as though a thousand words that should have passed between them remained unsaid.

*   *   *

Less than a week later, Caroline phoned the girl's home. She had tried her mobile but that had been switched off. Christine's mother explained that her daughter had gone to stay with friends for a few days. Caroline now knew the truth.

She sat alone and cried for Christine, for the baby and because of her own utter ineffectuality.

*   *   *

When Clive came in from work, he announced that David and Jenny Hines would be coming the following evening for their long-promised dinner.

Since Christine's departure, Clive had not alluded to her or to her relationship with Adam. It was as though she had never come in search of their son, or their help and understanding.

Knowing that the child was now lost—and not wishing to provoke more anger in her home about a problem which was past resolving—Caroline did not confide in Clive about Christine's decision. He never once asked the outcome of the girl's dilemma, so Caroline remained alone and lonely in her grief.

*   *   *

As she prepared the meal for their dinner guests and possibly because the thought of David Hines brought back memories of the evening at the golf club, Caroline's mind returned to Clive and Diane Tully. The matter of Christine and her baby had temporarily occupied her thoughts to such an extent that she had deferred the issue of Clive's infidelity to the back of her mind, where it hovered insidiously, awaiting the moment of its revival.

Once again, the agony of uncertainty took hold of Caroline's vulnerable being. It gripped her insides and twisted them cruelly into a tight and painful coil.

The idea of following Clive on his evenings out was anathema to her. Such deceit within marriage was unforgivable, yet his own behaviour, if indeed he was being unfaithful, was equally duplicitous.

Caroline felt that she could no longer remain ignorant of the truth. If he was having an affair, she had to know about it and to talk to him, in earnest, on the subject.

Hopefully, if confronted on the matter, he would give up his flighty young mistress and choose to stay with her. At least, then, she would no longer be considered a fool, someone easily deceived and gullible to the point of stupidity.

She was sure that she would be able to go on with their marriage if he was truly sorry— and if he finished the affair absolutely.

If he left her, though, and went off with youthful Diane . . . what then? Could she cope with a divorce and with living alone?

Caroline thought back, quite suddenly, to her father's death. She remembered her mother, soon after the funeral, cleaning the house from top to bottom and she recalled her words:

'If you keep your hands busy, Caroline,' her mother had said, 'it stops you thinking.'

At this moment Caroline needed, more than anything else, not to think. She blundered into the most complicated main course recipe that she could find, so dispelling Clive from her mind.

Well—almost.

*   *   *

As she changed her clothes, ready to receive her guests, Caroline knew that she would, once more, have to create the impression that all was well in the Marshall home.

She longed for the time when her contented behaviour on such occasions would truly reflect her state of mind, and when her thoughts would no longer be heavy with anxiety or anger or sorrow. True happiness, if she had ever really known it, seemed to belong to the past.

*   *   *

To Caroline's great relief, the food turned out to be superb, and the compliments from Jenny and David gave her spirits a much needed lift.

During the meal, the conversation drifted, in convivial manner, from the two men and their bank to Jenny's work in school and back again. In fact, if the food had not brought Caroline some recognition, she would have felt quite superfluous to the occasion.

When the business of eating had been dispensed with, Clive and David settled down in armchairs, each with a brandy, while Jenny helped Caroline to load the dishwasher and dispose of the debris which always materializes after a good meal.

Caroline noticed how swiftly Jenny moved around the kitchen; it was as though she wished to be economical with her movements. She was very slim and petite, and her short, blonde hair was styled to look business-like and chic.

'I do envy you, Caroline,' Jenny declared, as the two women tidied busily.

'Me?' Caroline asked, finding it inconceivable that anyone should find her life enviable, but realizing that she must be doing a competent impression of a contented wife and mother.

'Well, you're obviously so fulfilled. You know—your wonderful cooking and your lovely home—you seem to need nothing else. I wish I could be like that, but I've tried and I can't. It's probably a terrible admission to make but I get bored out of my mind if I stay at home. As it is, I'm exhausted most of the time because of the pressures at work. But I need my job—I enjoy it, I suppose.'

'Well, that's good, Jenny. It must be very rewarding to have an interesting and responsible job to do.'

'Do you think so?'

'Yes, of course. It makes you so much more complete—as a person. I feel . . . how can I put it? . . . insignificant when I'm with career women like you.'

'You shouldn't.'

'It isn't just that I don't seem to have anything of interest to talk about,' Caroline explained. 'It's a kind of alienation somehow. Like when you were talking in there about your work. You, David, and Clive are all wage-earners, and you'd be surprised how different I feel because I'm not.'

'Oh, Caroline, I'm sorry about that. I didn't realize.'

'I don't expect many people do. Don't envy me, though, Jenny. I wish I had the kind of independence that you've got—that earning your own salary brings.'

'What did you do before you married to Clive?'

'I was a boring old secretary; one of the millions who learned to type and do shorthand.'

'Well, you could get a job in an office— secretaries are always in demand.'

'The trouble with being a secretary is that there's a subservience attached to it. Do you know what I mean? One man's wife, another man's secretary . . . goodness, don't I sound sexist? But you're a skivvy for the important people, aren't you? They do the interesting work and make the decisions, whilst you do the boring, mindless bit.'

'It's still a job, though. It would surely give you some independence—and your own wages every month.'

'I shouldn't think I could do it now, anyway—what with computers and word processors—I'd be terrified!'

'No, you'd soon pick up the technology— really, there's nothing to it! If some of these wet-looking creatures you see in offices and banks can cope, I'm sure you could.'

Diane Tully sprang immediately to Caroline's mind. Yes, Jenny was surely right. If that dumb-looking blonde could hold down a job, she certainly could!

'I'll think it over, Caroline said, with just a hint of indignation, which Jenny, being unaware of her hostess's hatred of Miss Tully and her angry thoughts about same, feared was directed at her.

Once all four were reunited in the lounge, the topic of conversation altered as Jenny announced the plans for the Hines' summer holiday.

'My parents are coming to stay with Angela,' she explained, 'so that David and I can get away on our own. We're going on safari in Kenya.'

'Where do your parents live, Jenny?' Caroline inquired.

'Down on the south coast. They retired there a couple of years ago.'

'You're so lucky to have them both,' Caroline enthused. 'We lost my dad, when he was only in his fifties, and my mum lives alone.'

'She's used to that, though, I suppose,' David said. 'It's all right if they're fit, isn't it?'

'Well, she's rather overweight, I'm afraid,' Caroline replied, as though her mother's plumpness were her fault. 'She doesn't eat too much or anything like that . . . she just can't seem to lose it. The trouble is, she can't get around like she used to. Her neighbours pop in every day, and she's got the phone, of course, but it's still a bit of a worry.'

'Have you suggested that old people's home to her yet, Caro?' Clive asked.

'No. I don't know how she'd feel about that.'

'I know it must be difficult,' Jenny agreed, 'but it's the only answer really, isn't it? If she's reached the stage where you don't feel she's safe on her own, then get her into somewhere where she'll have constant supervision. It would be a load off your mind, wouldn't it?'

Caroline nodded, but Jenny's words hung uncomfortably in her mind. Yes, she mused, glancing at Jenny, David, and Clive in turn; none of these go-getters would have any doubts, would they? Put mother in a home and then we can forget about her . . . apart from the duty visits, of course. Yes . . . let's get on with our careers. Let's plan the holidays, build a swimming pool and landscape the bloody garden!

'You look miles away, Caroline,' David remarked. 'Are you all right?'

'Sorry? Yes . . . sorry, I was . . . er . . . I was thinking about Peggy, my friend from next door.' Caroline felt that she should say no more about her mother at present. 'She's had cancer,' she continued, 'in the breast. She had to have it removed.'

'Oh, how ghastly!' Jenny exclaimed. 'The thought of it terrifies me—I don't mind admitting it.'

'Yes, me too,' Caroline answered emphatically. 'She's got to have some follow-up treatment, but they think she'll be all right.'

'Some people are so brave about things like that, aren't they?' Jenny went on. 'I'm an absolute coward. Did she have the whole breast removed?'

'Yes, I'm afraid she did.' Caroline's eyes found Clive's as she spoke. 'She's quite badly scarred, I believe.'

83

'Of course,' Jenny said, as though the idea of scars was a new one to her, 'as if it's not enough to have to cope with the illness, you've got the awful marks on your body—especially when it's that part of the body. No more bikinis, eh?'

'I don't think that will worry Peggy too much,' Caroline replied, just a little sharply.

'Don't you think it must be difficult for the husband, too?' Clive suddenly put in, addressing his question to David. 'I'm sure Caro thinks I'm heartless because I admitted that I'd find that kind of mutilation rather repulsive. Now, be honest, David, wouldn't you be put off by scars like that?'

'I've never thought about it,' David answered, looking more than a little uncomfortable.

'Yes, well, let's just hope that none of us ever has to cope with such an awful problem,' Jenny said, determined to change the subject. 'Now, where are you two going for your holiday this year?'

'Italy,' Clive replied, clearly annoyed that David had not answered his question in the way that he had hoped he would.

'We're going in November,' Caroline added, 'when Adam is back at college . . . we don't like travelling when it's really hot and crowded.'

Caroline was looking forward to seeing Venice; its uniqueness had always attracted

84

and fascinated her.

There was a lull in the conversation. Caroline thought of Italy. She prayed that by the time their holiday arrived, the recent doubts and complications in her life would be banished, so that she could go with a light heart and a free mind.

*   *   *

When Jenny and David had left, Caroline went quickly to bed. She felt exhausted by the company, or rather, by the performance she had been obliged to give.

The night was hot and humid and, as Caroline enjoyed the coolness of the sheets, she allowed the tension to fall from her limbs and neck. She was soon asleep. Unfortunately, though, she was not to have the rest she so needed.

There, as the blackness of the night and the depths of her innermost mind converged, the world of Caroline's sub-conscious struggled for domination.

She saw, in what seemed like a huge, muddy battlefield, row upon row of babies—newborn babies. They were all exactly the same . . . naked, with eyes that cried, and mouths stretched wide from silent screaming. Then, a mist, a thick, impenetrable mist began to rise from the uneven surface of the black field. It swirled slowly around each tiny body, and, as it drifted upward, it left only skeletons in its wake.

Caroline sat up in bed and, though she opened her eyes in an attempt to rid her mind of the horrifying picture that had broken her sleep, the dream lingered, hideous and shocking in its clarity. She was clammy and breathless. Clive was sleeping soundly and, as she crept to the bathroom, Caroline wished that she could wake him and tell him of her nightmare, but she could not.

Relief came as the bathroom light restored reality to her eyes. She stooped over the wash basin and splashed her face with cold water. Her hands still trembled.

'Now, Caroline Marshall,' she said firmly, looking at herself in the mirror, 'you've got to get a hold of yourself.'

After patting her face and neck with a towel, she drank some water and took a Valium. These little white pills had been her intermittent comforters for some time now.

Caroline slipped back into bed. She found solace in Clive's strong, warm body next to her and, though she could not talk to him about her terrible dream, she was glad that he was there.

As she waited for the tranquilizer to bring serene slumber, Caroline reflected, once again, on the matter of Christine's abortion. Why, she wondered, did she feel guilt about it all? If she had offered a home to the girl and

86

her baby, it would probably have been refused. For goodness sake, she applauded the various freedoms which women were gradually gaining and the ability to determine what happens to one's own body is surely the most fundamental of freedoms. She should not begrudge Christine the opportunity to start again; the chance to eradicate the one mistake which has ruined the lives of so many women through the ages, yet so often left the men involved relatively, sometimes totally, unscathed. No, it was over-emotional to think of the baby at that early stage—it was not really so much different from taking the pill and she had been obliged to do that herself for many years.

Looking at it practically, Christine had probably made the right decision. The most important thing being that it had been her own decision. Adam would probably have agreed anyway, if he had been around.

Caroline rested her head against Clive's shoulder and, as she found deep, dreamless sleep, she wished that she could always feel this close to him. His renewed consciousness, though, would bring with it the usual discord and tension.

CHAPTER TEN

The morning found Caroline feeling rather more in control than she had done for some time. It seemed that she had rationalized Christine's decision about the abortion and found an uneasy acceptance of the situation.

Grey clouds hung heavily in the sky, and the humidity of the previous night had spilled into the new day. Even the slightest exertion drained Caroline's energy.

She watched, from the lounge window, for Steven to bring Peggy home from the hospital. Once she had seen him go back to work, she would go next door and help Peggy to settle in.

It was late morning when Steven drove away, and Caroline wasted no time in taking a welcome home card and an African violet—in vivid, purple bloom—to her best friend.

Peggy looked a little pale but was elated to be back home.

'Thanks for keeping an eye on Steven and the twins, Caroline,' she said. 'It was a wonderful help to know that they were eating properly and being kept in some sort of order.'

'Don't be silly, Peggy—I enjoyed it. And I know you'd do the same for me.'

'Here's hoping that I never have to,' Peggy replied solemnly. Then, instantly brightening again, she continued, 'I can't tell you how lovely it is to be home again!'

'And you're feeling well?'

'Yes, I am, thanks. I know it sounds a bit corny,' Peggy went on, as the two women settled down for a chat, 'but being in hospital has given me lots of time to think. Perhaps it's because I've had cancer as well, I don't know, but I made my mind up, lying there, that from now on I'm going to make the most of every day I'm given. I'm going to do things that I've always wanted to. For a start, I'm going to buy an easel, canvas, and hundreds of oils, and I'm going to take up painting.'

'I never knew you were interested in art!'

'No, you didn't, and that's exactly my point! From now on, if my bedrooms need to be sorted out—or even if the whole wretched house wants a good cleaning—but it's a beautiful day and I feel like painting, I shall go out to the countryside, or into the garden, and I'll paint a picture! To hell with the housework! And if I fancy a day in London browsing round the galleries—or Paris, even— I shall go! I know I'm not house proud, but I've still spent too much time doing what I've had to and not nearly enough doing what I've wanted to. And all that's going to change now. It might be fun to go to one or two of those adult education courses, too—pottery or something.'

'I've been thinking of changing my life, too, though not in the same way as you.' Caroline spoke tentatively, as though unsure of her aspirations.

'Really? How?'

'I thought I might try to get a job—secretarial work, like I used to do.'

'Yes, why not?'

'It isn't that I need the money. I've absolutely no complaints about Clive in that direction. He's always bought me anything I've asked for. I just feel that I want a change; it would be a challenge, too. I'd meet different people and I'd have something to think about other than Clive, Adam and the house.'

'I know what you mean.'

'It isn't that I don't care about the family. I just feel that I need more now—an extra interest. I would like to be more independent too, and it would be good to have my own money and not have to ask Clive for everything.'

'Well, I hope you get a really super job, Caroline; it would do you the world of good. I'm sure of it.'

'Yes, I think it might. David and Jenny Hines came to dinner last night,' Caroline went on, 'You know, Clive's assistant manager . . . and his wife is a teacher.'

'Oh, yes, I've heard you mention them before.'

'Well, she's a real career woman—after a headship—you know the type. Anyway, she seems so . . . so self-confident and efficient . . .

not in a nasty way, just very competent. I've always envied women like that and I want to prove to myself that I can be like them. For goodness sake, Peggy, if I can't do it now that Adam is grown up and with Mrs. Curran to do the housework too, well, I might as well resign myself to the fact that I'm good for nothing— except cooking and living on reflected glory from Clive!'

What Caroline had omitted to confess to either Peggy or Jenny Hines was that these career women, of whom she now spoke, had always intimidated her. Their strength, and their obvious confidence in their own words and deeds, almost frightened her. In the past she had found compensation in the fact that she had thought of such women as being pressured into their way of life. Perhaps by the need for money, the quest for equality with men or the numerous social demands, which were heaped upon them merely because they were living in the twenty first century. Previously, she had felt fortunate that she had never succumbed to such pressures and she had told herself that she pitied those who had. Though she knew that what she truly felt was fear—fear born from the supposition that she would always live a life so different from theirs, that the secret force which fed their strength would always be denied to her.

Perhaps now, even if her world did prove to be mundane, and her salary comparatively poor, she would find, at least, some measure of the self-possession and boldness which she had always lacked.

*   *   *

When Clive returned home from work, Caroline was writing letters of application for secretarial posts, which she had seen advertised. She had made up her mind that she would tell Clive of her decision to look for employment, rather than to ask for his approval.

'It isn't anything really to do with money,' she explained to him, 'you've never kept me short of cash. But I'd like another interest, now that Adam's left home.'

'Good idea,' Clive interrupted, making the speech of persuasion, which Caroline had rehearsed over and over again in her mind, quite unnecessary.

'Oh, do you think so?' she asked, with both delight and surprise in her voice.

'Yes. Give it a whirl—see how it goes. If it doesn't work out you can always give notice.'

'Well . . . yes . . . that's exactly it. I thought I'd just give it a try.'

'Good.' Clive seemed in a hurry. 'I'll go and shower, then. It's squash tonight. Is dinner nearly ready?'

Caroline put stamps on her letters of application and then went to the kitchen to finish preparing the meal.

She was relieved that Clive had not raised objections to her plans. He had, in fact, seemed rather uninterested. It was not the reaction she had expected at all. Perhaps he was too pre-occupied with his forthcoming squash to give her very much attention. Or was it another kind of 'sport' he was so looking forward to?

'I've promised to pick up one of the reserves on the way there,' he explained, as he rushed his meal.

'Anyone I know?'

'Peter—Peter Stanford. No, you don't know him.'

'And where does he live?'

'The new estate—St James's Avenue. Why?'

'I just wondered.'

Caroline was suspicious.

*　　　*　　　*

She sat contemplating what his evening might really hold in store. She saw him, in her mind's eye, greeting Diane Tully with an embrace that revealed that affection as well as passion was present in their illicit relationship.

A destructive fury grew within her. There was no warning; it was suddenly there—a burning, tormenting anger. The control she had found earlier in the day had deserted her now. All thoughts of a job had vanished. All she could think of was Clive—and that girl.

She felt suffocated by the heat of the kitchen. Throwing open the back door, she rushed into the garden in search of fresh air, but she found only sticky, heady stillness.

Caroline felt that she was choking; she could not rid her mind of the vision of Clive holding that girl in his arms. The agony of the jealousy and the pain of the betrayal were more real to her now than ever before. Her inflamed emotions seemed to be pushing, from the centre of her being, upward to her throat. She hurried to the lounge and poured herself a whisky.

Then, quite suddenly, she knew what to do. Before she had had time to question her decision and bombard herself with the usual self-doubts, Caroline was in her car and driving towards Poplar Close.

Her hands clutched the steering wheel tightly and sweat from her trembling fingers moistened its shiny surface. She must have driven completely from instinct and habit because, as she turned into Poplar Close, Caroline had no recollection of the short journey she had just made.

The road was wide and the houses on either side were large and detached. Caroline drove slowly, peering into each driveway.

Clive's car was not there.

She stopped at the end of this lavish close and turned off the engine. Should she wait there in case he arrived later in the evening. Perhaps he had planned to visit his mistress after his game of squash.

Caroline wondered which house was Diane Tully's.

She sat there convincing herself that her suspicions were founded on fact. What other reason would Clive have to be in Poplar Close the night that June had seen him? He must have been with Diane Tully. He must have been!

After a few minutes, during which she took some deep breaths and calmed herself somewhat, Caroline decided to leave. Instead of driving straight home, however, she went first to the squash club.

Clive's car was there, in the car park.

There was some strange relief in knowing that, at least, he was not with his mistress—in her house—in her bedroom—at that moment.

Caroline drove home again. She was unsure whether or not she would visit Poplar Close again later that night.

Her mind was made up for her, though, when she opened the front door and found Adam's luggage sitting in the hall.

'Hello, mum!' he called from upstairs. 'I ran out of money so I had to come home!'

Caroline found immediate comfort in hearing her son's voice.

CHAPTER ELEVEN

Adam's tan and unshaven face made him look even more handsome than when he had gone away.

Caroline cooked him a hot meal while he told her about the highlights of his weeks in France. Then, as he began to eat, she broached the subject that had caused her so much distress. She was apprehensive and troubled. His mood was so bright and oozing with youthful freedom that it seemed almost a criminal act to change it.

'Someone came to see you while you were away, Adam,' she began.

'Jimmy Parsons? He said he might come and visit, but I told him to phone first to make sure I was back from France . . . he is a . . .'

'No, Adam . . . it was a girl.'

'Oh—who?'

It was evident that no one in particular had sprung to mind.

'Christine . . . Christine Jordan.'

'Oh, her.' Adam sounded disappointed.

'Yes, she wanted to see you.'

'Honestly, some girls! What the hell do you have to do to shake them off? At the end of term I had all the guys lying for me while I hid from Miss Christine Jordan. She must have realized that I was avoiding her, surely. I hope she's not stalking me now.'

'So, you're not . . . er . . . keen on her?'

'No, I'm not!'

'Adam . . .' Caroline paused.

'Mm?'

'Adam, Christine was expecting your baby.'

'What? The stupid cow!'

'Adam!' Caroline was horrified.

'Well, for God's sake, mum! I thought she was on the pill!'

'Why did you think that? Did she tell you she was?'

'No. But she didn't tell me she wasn't, either! What am I, a mind reader? Look . . . if a girl doesn't ask me to take precautions, I presume she has!'

'Adam! You're talking as though you've been . . . well . . . sleeping around! Have you lived your entire life oblivious to AIDS and the warnings about other sexually transmitted diseases? Pregnancy isn't the only thing to be avoided!'

'No, I haven't! Look, mum, I don't exactly have a different girl every night, but I haven't taken holy orders, either. Christine is the only girl I've had unprotected sex with. These things happen . . . but I honestly thought she was on the pill!'

Caroline rubbed her forehead with her fingertips; she felt that she no longer knew Adam.

'So, you're obviously not in love with

Christine?'

'Hell, no!'

'But you told her you loved her.'

'Yes . . . I probably did.'

'So you were lying.'

'Mum! Do I have to draw a picture? There are times when you say things that seem appropriate at that moment but they aren't necessarily gospel!'

'Christine believed you.'

'Well, she must be pretty bloody naïve!'

'She loves you, Adam.' Caroline was desperately trying to be patient.

'I can't help that. It's her own fault for taking it all so bloody seriously.'

'I told her you'd phone her when you got home.'

'Oh, Christ!'

'She tried to see you—to talk to you about the baby. She was very upset about it all; she's a sensitive girl, you know.'

'I'll phone her sometime—maybe.'

'No, Adam—you'll phone her tonight!' Caroline had rarely shown authority when talking to her son, but now her face was stern and her voice commanding. 'Don't you understand?' she shouted. 'Christine isn't one of these trendy young things who's out for sexual encounters and nothing more! She was too busy innocently loving you to think in practical terms! You, on the other hand, clearly know what you're doing, and should

98

have known better than to assume that it was safe to have sex!'

'All right, mum! Calm down, will you?'

'No, I won't calm down! That girl has had an abortion! She's got rid of her child—your child—God knows what mental anguish she's been going through! It's probably scarred her emotionally and she'll stay that way for the rest of her life! But you! It's all just a bloody nuisance to you, isn't it?'

'I'm going out!'

'Where?'

'For a walk! Don't wait up!'

Adam was gone.

Caroline slumped into a chair and cried. Her son was now a man. She had accepted that, but his attitude towards that poor girl . . . his heartlessness and his obvious permissiveness, too . . . these things she could not come to terms with. He had always been such a caring, sensitive boy. How could he have changed so much, and so quickly?

It seemed that another part of her life, a part in which she had felt safe, was falling away from her, to leave her vulnerable and insecure. Adam was a stranger now and one that she was not sure she could like.

As he had talked of Christine's stupidity and naïveté, Caroline had seen Clive in his eyes. The realization that his views were very much as his father's had been was a shock that Caroline could not absorb.

* * *

Clive was later than usual.

As she waited for him, Caroline could not bear to think of where he might be—or even worse—whom he might be with. It was equally painful for her to consider Adam and the row they had had. Her heart went out to Christine.

She wanted to sleep. To be conscious and to be aware was insufferable to her; she could stand no more reality that night. The answer came in the form of a tranquilizer, which she took before going despondent and alone to her bed.

She did not hear Clive or Adam come home but in the morning, her husband was beside her when she woke.

'I see Adam's arrived,' he said sleepily, as Caroline forced open her eyes. 'Is he all right? I didn't think he'd be back so soon.'

'He's fine,' she replied, closing her eyes again.

Caroline stayed in bed, allowing Adam and Clive time on their own. She did not know whether they would speak about Christine and the baby, or if Adam would tell his father about the row of the previous night . . . and just now, she did not care.

It was quiet and comfortable, lying there. Caroline felt safe—protected somehow from her worries by the semi-conscious state she was in. She did not want to feel wide awake, so she kept her eyes shut and dozed until the Valium had worn off completely and she could postpone the day no longer.

As she came down the stairs, she heard Clive and Adam talking in the kitchen.

'. . . I don't expect you to live like a monk,' Clive was saying, 'but for Christ's sake, use your head, son.'

Caroline sank down onto the stairs; she felt compelled to listen.

'Yes, all right, dad. Don't go on.'

'You've got to be careful. Even if they tell you they're on the pill, you've got to take precautions. Some girls will lie so that they'll get pregnant and make you their meal ticket for life—and to hell with your prospects and your career! Let this be a lesson to you.'

Caroline's finger nails dug into the palms of her hands. She was seething. She wondered how much of Clive's knowledge of such matters was born from first hand experience.

'All right, dad, I'll be careful in future. Can we forget it now?'

'I don't think you realize the trouble you could have caused,' Clive went on. 'Your mother only wanted the damned girl and her kid to come and live with us. I was supposed to help finance them.'

'What?'

'Yes . . . you know what your mother's like. She could see us all as one big happy family.

Can you imagine it?'

'Mm. Pure hell!'

'Exactly. She wanted us to look after what's her name and the baby until you could get married and afford your own place.'

'Married?' Adam was clearly horrified 'Poor old mum—she hasn't got a clue, has she? She was going on about love last night. I should have guessed she was hearing wedding bells.'

'I haven't mentioned any of this since the girl went back home. I should imagine she's had an abortion, otherwise your mother would still have been bending my ear about it.'

'She has. Mum told me last night that Christine has had an abortion.'

'Thank God the girl has some sense!'

Caroline could listen to no more of this. She crept back upstairs and ran a bath.

They were two of a kind, Clive and Adam. These men who had been the most important people in her life for so long. They spoke the same language—a language that was foreign and repugnant to her. Caroline soaked herself in the steaming hot bath. She no longer felt like the linchpin of her little family—no, she was the outsider, the one to be ridiculed. How dare they be so patronizing towards her?

'I wonder how you would have behaved if we'd had a daughter, Clive Marshall,' she whispered. 'What fatherly advice would you have given her?'

It was Saturday and Clive spent the morning in the garden. Though it was a mystery to Caroline what he found to do out there for so long, she was glad that she did not have to converse with him.

Adam went into town and reappeared at lunchtime.

By the afternoon, Clive had settled down to watch sport on the television and Caroline took Adam to visit her mother. It had been several days since she had last seen her.

'I'm sorry about last night, mum,' Adam began hesitantly, as the car left the driveway.

'Let's forget it, shall we?' Caroline answered sharply.

'I think that people of your age look at things differently,' Adam went on.

'Of my age!' Caroline gasped. 'I'm not eligible for my bus-pass yet, Adam!'

'No, I know, mum. I didn't mean that you're old, but your generation does see things in a different way, doesn't it?'

'Rubbish!' Caroline snapped. 'Your father is the same age as me, but he appeared to view the situation in exactly the same way as you. On the other hand, Christine—your generation, remember—was affected very much as I would have been. I don't think that age is the problem, do you?'

'Perhaps not. It's all over now, though, isn't

103

it? If we row about it for the next month, it won't alter what's happened. I'll contact Christine, I promise, but there's no hurry.'

'Well, if that's what you've decided Adam, you must do what you think is right.'

The subject was dropped. Caroline did not want to argue any further with Adam. Her state of mind would not stand it. She needed to encourage calmness in her life, of that she was certain.

Clive's infidelity would also remain a taboo subject while Adam stayed at home. Caroline did not want an atmosphere of contention between herself and Clive, which would erupt into a row whenever Adam left the house, and decline into a silent sulk whenever he returned. That would not be fair.

Once Adam had gone back to college, though, she would have to decide what to do about her ailing marriage. For the sake of sanity, however, the deferment of this major decision, and the crisis that would almost certainly follow, was a much-needed respite.

CHAPTER TWELVE

At nine o'clock on the following Tuesday morning, Caroline was already seated in the hairdresser's.

'Thanks for fitting me in at such short

notice,' she said to June, 'but I need to look a bit special today.'

'Going somewhere exciting?'

'I don't know if you'd say that exactly—I've got an interview for a job this afternoon.'

'Really? Where?'

'Grainger's, the electronics place in Market Street. I'll be working in the office, doing secretarial stuff. It's the only thing I'm trained to do. I didn't get the letter till yesterday, though. They don't believe in giving people much time, do they?'

'I can't say that I blame you, Mrs. Marshall. Now that your son's off getting himself a life, you might as well get out and do something for yourself. Being a housewife must be boring . . . lots of my ladies say it is, anyway.'

'Yes, I do feel I need an interest outside of the house.'

'Has your son gone back to college yet?'

'No, not till the beginning of October.'

'It must be lovely to have him at home.' Caroline was unaware that her face had clouded as Adam was spoken of. 'You look worried, Mrs Marshall,' June continued. 'In fact, if you don't mind me saying so, you really haven't looked well for weeks now. You seem sort of anxious all the time. Is everything all right?'

'Oh, dear, is it that obvious?'

'Not to the casual observer, maybe, but I've known you for such a long time. You get close to people in this job. Well, I do, anyway.'

'Adam is worrying me a bit, if I'm honest.'

'I'm sorry to hear that. Not in any kind of trouble, is he?'

'No, no . . . it's nothing like that. It's his attitude to life, really. He seems to have changed a lot since he went to university.'

'That's bound to happen, though. He's still young and trying to find his way in life.'

'Yes, I expected him to grow away from us, to become a man, but . . . he seems to have lost the caring side of his character. He's become insensitive.'

'Oh, I see.'

It was apparent to Caroline that June did not really see at all.

'When you bring up a child, you surround it with love,' Caroline explained. 'You hope . . . no . . . more than that . . . you expect it to grow up to be a loving, caring person, and I don't think Adam has . . . and that hurts . . . it hurts more than you can imagine.'

'It makes me thankful I don't have any of my own,' June declared. 'So many of my ladies say the same sort of thing about their children, and when they're not moaning about their kids, it's their husbands.'

Caroline smiled weakly.

'So you're not on the look-out for Mr. Right, then?'

'No, definitely not. To tell you the truth, Mrs. Marshall, I don't think I could live with a

106

man—not now. I'm too used to my independence. When I see some of my married friends and the mess their lives are in, I thank the Lord that I'm single.'

'Do you not get lonely?' Caroline asked, with thoughts of her own future very much in her mind.

'No, I do what I like when I like. I have no one to please but myself. I've got loads of friends and lots of hobbies, too. Never a dull moment, as they say.'

'What about boyfriends?'

'I go out with men sometimes and I quite enjoy their company, but I can't honestly say that I've ever met one I wanted to spend the next few months with, let alone the rest of my life. To be truthful, I find that most men are extremely full of themselves—do you know what I mean?'

'Mm.' Caroline knew exactly what June meant.

'They sit there talking about themselves all the time, what they like, what they don't like, where they've been, what they've done, and how brilliant they are at golf or cricket or whatever, and you're supposed to be fascinated by all this boring old rot. But if you talk for more than five minutes about yourself, they just give you a patronizing grin, and start to undress you with their eyes. They're not interested in us as people, are they?'

'I think some men are, June,' she replied,

wondering, at the same time, why she was arguing against a woman who was voicing a view which she herself had come to hold more and more strongly over the years.

'Well, I haven't met one yet who truly sees past your body to your mind.'

There was a pause and Caroline thought back to her youth.

'I don't think men were always so selfish and obsessed with sex,' she reflected. 'My father, for instance, was a very moral man. He was quite strict with me, but I knew it was because he feared for my safety. I wasn't allowed to drink or stay out late, and he vetted any boys who took me out on dates. I didn't really mind, at the time, because I knew why he was being over-protective, and he was such a good, kind man. I always had a great deal of respect for my father. He applied his rules to himself as well as to me. He didn't drink or gamble, and as for deceiving my mother— perish the thought! You could trust him totally and depend on him in any circumstances— he'd never let you down. He was a rock and I always felt so safe, so secure, when he was there.'

'Perhaps you saw him through a daughter's eyes rather than a wife's or a woman's eyes. I mean, your mother might have seen him quite differently, being married to him.'

'I don't think she did, June.'

Caroline admired her finished hairstyle.

'I hope your problems with your son soon pass,' June said quietly, as she handed Caroline her change from the till.

'Thanks. If they don't, I shall have to learn to cope with them. I seem to be doing a lot of coping recently.'

'You do sound so low,' June sympathized.

'Take no notice—I've not been myself recently. I'm hoping that getting a job will help matters and give me a new lease of life. I've been feeling there's a lid, where the top of my head should be, and it's as though someone is screwing it down tighter and tighter. Does that sound stupid?'

'It sounds ghastly! Good luck with your interview this afternoon—and I hope it helps you to feel like your old self again!'

*   *   *

As the appointed time of her interview approached, Caroline began to feel nervous. She would not get the job; she was absolutely certain of that. They would ask her to type a sample letter and she had not touched a keyboard for years. She would have practised, but there was so little notice, and if they asked her to demonstrate her skills on a computer, she would have to admit that she knew very little about them. She could barely turn on the one at home without Clive's assistance.

Suddenly there seemed to be no point at all

in going, yet, at quarter to two, she was walking into Grainger's in a stylish navy blue suit and smart, white blouse.

She was shown into a waiting room, where she sat alone for only a few moments before another candidate was shown in and then another.

A number of glances, but no conversation, passed between the three hopeful applicants.

Caroline, in her hurried appraisal of her two opponents, guessed that they were both in their early twenties and positively oozing with qualifications. Why was she subjecting herself to this ordeal? She had no hope of getting the job; she was becoming more certain of that with each passing second.

Both the younger women, sitting opposite her, looked as though they had never been nervous about anything in their lives. Caroline, however, was sure that her present fear was spread over her face for all to see. Her fingers refused to be still on her lap, instead they hovered and danced about completely out of her control.

She felt quite aged in the company of these confident young women and longed to crawl, unseen, out of the building and forget all about her recent aspirations to obtain work.

'Mrs. Marshall,' a voice said clearly. There was no turning back. Caroline was shown into the manager's office.

* * *

'It was awful, Peggy!' Caroline gasped, as she drank a very welcome and comforting cup of tea. 'They asked me to type a piece of work and I took ages over it. Then they asked if I'd ever used Word, Excel, or PowerPoint. I had no idea what they were talking about. I had to say no. That's it—finished! I'll forget all about a job—it was a stupid idea, anyway, and I never want to go through that again!'

'Oh, Caroline, don't be put off because it went wrong today,' Peggy pleaded. 'Practise your typing and improve your speed. Get Clive to show you how to use a computer properly. Maybe he could even take you into the bank for a bit of work experience before you go for your next interview.'

'No,' Caroline replied, with uncharacteristic resolve, which quite startled Peggy. 'No, I don't want to go to the bank, and I don't want Clive to teach me anything!'

'Well, all right, just improve your typing,' Peggy replied quietly, hoping to placate Caroline. 'There must still be offices where they want a good short-hand typist, surely.'

'I'll see . . . perhaps,' was all the agreement that Caroline would offer.

* * *

Clive did not ask about the outcome of her

interview, so Caroline guessed that he had attached so little importance to the event that he had forgotten all about it. As it was not an afternoon about which she wished to boast, or indeed to elucidate in any way, Caroline decided that she would not mention it either.

Whether or not she would attend another interview, she did not know. She would decide if the opportunity arose, but for the time being, Caroline chose to ignore even the possibility of such an ordeal.

*   *   *

The builders arrived to begin work on the indoor swimming pool, the following morning.

Caroline watched as men and machines assembled together and began to scoop out the ground at one side of the house.

'It'll be great when it's built, won't it, mum?' Adam enthused, as he joined her in the garden. 'You'll be able to have pool parties!'

'Yes, I suppose we will,' was Caroline's flat reply. 'I'll see you later, Adam. I'm going to visit your grandmother—I feel I've been neglecting her lately.'

CHAPTER THIRTEEN

As work progressed on the swimming pool, Caroline watched more with contempt than interest or enthusiasm.

Each day, she took her typewriter down from the loft and spent an hour improving her speed. Although she had been discouraged by her first interview, after a few days and the initial trauma of the experience had passed, Caroline decided that it would be cowardly of her to declare that she would never try again. This submissive attitude was largely what she was attempting to rid herself of, so she must summon her courage and give herself a better chance of success next time.

It was two weeks after her first interview that her second appointment arrived through the post.

This time she was more eager to get the job. The advertisement had said that an old, established firm of solicitors required a competent short-hand typist, and Caroline felt that she would be more suited to this kind of work than that offered by larger concerns, such as Grainger's Electronics.

On the day of the interview, Caroline made herself look as business-like and professional as possible. She felt more confident than before and some measure of determination could be detected in her manner as she went about her preparations.

It was Clive she had to thank for this added drive. He had not only neglected to ask about the outcome of her first interview, but had also failed to mention her quest for employment in any way. It was obvious that he had set little store in her ability to join, or sustain a place in, the working world and, because of his attitude, Caroline had resolved to prove him wrong. Clive's silence had presented her with a far stronger challenge than any arguments against her working could have done.

Robertson & Allsworth's office was situated near the centre of town. The smell of old papers produced a mustiness that could not be overlooked as one entered the hall of the Victorian house.

Caroline was interviewed by two elderly gentlemen, each with grey hair and a moustache. They looked like brothers but one was Mr. Robertson and the other Mr. Allsworth. They were very courteous, and Caroline was enchanted, both by their extreme politeness and the general atmosphere of the house, which she felt must be reminiscent of the early nineteen hundreds. Indeed, the two old gentlemen would not have been out of place in a Dickens' novel.

She was not asked to type a sample letter. She was not even asked what her speed was and, though they did wish to see her references, when she explained that she had none because she had not worked for many years, they were quite happy to offer Caroline employment.

Mr. Allsworth explained that they wanted a more mature lady, as they had found some younger ladies to be rather unreliable; at which point Mr. Robertson emphasized that they did not wish to offend by implying that she was not young. Caroline assured them that she understood perfectly and she left the office delighted that she had got a job—no—she had secured a position, in a place where she had felt instantly at home—a cosy, gentle place.

Clive looked a little surprised when Caroline told him about her new employment. This was nothing, though, compared to the utter dismay he exhibited when she explained that she had not asked what her salary would be, as the subject of money was not raised, and would have seemed somehow obscene in such a genteel interview.

*   *   *

When Caroline started work the following Monday, she was not disappointed. Entering Robertson & Allsworth's was like stepping out of this century and back to a time long past and forgotten.

There were four solicitors in the firm: the

elderly Mr. Allsworth and the equally elderly Mr. Robertson, along with Mr. Robertson's son, who was introduced to Caroline as Mr. Geoffrey and Mr. Barker, a trainee in his mid-twenties.

'For goodness sake, call me Geoff,' Mr. Robertson junior insisted, with a pleasantly warm smile, when he and Caroline were alone. 'You mustn't mind father and Uncle Teddy—they tend to cling to the past, but you'll find they're good employers.'

'I think it's enchanting,' Caroline replied in awe, 'but that's probably because the present day doesn't suit me very well—not everything about it does, anyway.'

Geoff smiled at her and Caroline found herself staring into his kind, blue eyes for far too long.

Geoffrey Robertson was in his early thirties. He was a tall, broad man with sandy hair and, though his features were not classically handsome, there was a serenity and warmth about his face, which was attractive and Caroline felt totally at ease in his presence.

'I'm trying to drag the business into the twenty first century,' he explained. 'There's a computer in that huge box over there and when I get round to unpacking it, I thought you might teach me how to use it.'

'Oh dear, you've asked the wrong person,' murmured Caroline. 'I haven't got a clue about such things.'

'Oh good! That IS refreshing!' Geoff beamed. 'I thought I was the only person born after the Second World War who found such things alien. Great! We'll learn to use it together . . . when I get round to unpacking it.'

'Mr. Barker would probably know all about computers—he's just the right age for them, I should think.'

'No . . . we've got the instruction manual . . . we'll fathom it out.'

Caroline smiled. She wondered if the business would ever be modernized; she doubted it. To be honest she hoped it would stay exactly as it was. She already loved the place.

The pace of the work was not hurried and she soon became accustomed to the daily routine. After a very short time, Caroline truly looked forward to coming into the office each morning.

Though Geoff's father and his uncle—his mother's brother—were the senior partners, they were gradually transferring the bulk of the business to Geoff and it was with him that Caroline spent most of her working day. The young Mr. Barker worked with the two elderly partners, learning his chosen profession conscientiously.

Geoff was a very placid man with a lively wit and Caroline found herself laughing more than she had done for many years.

Very soon, she came to realize that her

happiest hours were spent at work.

Clive was occasionally put out if his dinner was not ready at the usual time, especially if this meant that he was late for golf or squash, but Caroline did not care. She was beginning to live more for her work than for her family.

*   *   *

At the beginning of October, Adam returned to Cambridge. He told his mother that he had phoned Christine, but did not confide in her about their conversation.

Though, as usual, she felt a pang of sorrow to see Adam leave, Caroline did not experience the same sense of emptiness as she had done at his previous departures. No, Adam had his own life to lead. He must make his way in the world and she would not cling to him. She no longer wanted to.

*   *   *

Caroline found herself spending more and more time talking to Geoff. They had much in common and he seemed truly interested in her views on just about everything. She never spoke about her home life to Geoff. He knew that she was married with a teenage son, but she elucidated no further. She preferred, and intended, to keep her home life and her working life in completely separate compartments.

Geoff was a bachelor. He was not a sportsman, neither was he a man who enjoyed a hectic social life and, though he described himself as very dull, Caroline saw a depth of understanding in his character which exposed a caring and considerate man.

'Don't a lot of people get divorced?' Caroline remarked, as she attempted to get the clients' files into a more comprehensible system of classification.

'Yes, we're never short of work on that front. Puts you off marriage, really.'

'That's a shame.'

'Why do you say that?'

'I don't know . . . you're the sort of man who should be married.'

'Why?' he laughed. 'Do I look as though I need taking in hand?'

'No, but you'd make someone a smashing husband.'

'Don't you believe it.'

'Have you . . . I mean . . . is there someone special, Geoff?'

He stopped writing and looked forlornly across the room to where Caroline was ankle-deep in dusty files.

'Not now,' he answered, 'there was someone, a year or two back . . . but things didn't work out.'

'I'm sorry.' Caroline wished that she hadn't been so curious.

'All for the best,' Geoff went on. 'No good finding out you're not suited when you're married with a couple of kids—like most of those poor devils.'

He pointed at the files.

'That's true, I suppose.'

'Elly and I—we wouldn't have lasted long as a couple,' Geoff explained dreamily, his pen tapping gently and rhythmically against his lower lip. 'She was the ambitious type. Money was her business. She lives in London now, I believe. She's something big in the city, as they say. Lovely girl—very good-looking—I used to wonder what she saw in me . . . not much, obviously! She found me very dull after the initial novelty of the relationship had worn off and I found her social life exhausting. Chalk and cheese, we were.'

'What a shame.'

'She didn't really want to change her lifestyle at all. She expected me to accommodate her all the time. No give and take. If we had married, she would never have been at home—not that I wanted to tie her to the kitchen sink or anything like that—but companionship is part of the deal, isn't it?'

'Yes, an important part too.'

'The pace of Elly's life, compared to mine, would have set us on a collision course and neither of us was prepared to alter things—not enough, anyway.'

'I'm sorry—I shouldn't have asked,'

120

Caroline said apologetically.

'Not at all—it's good to talk about such things sometimes. It's all in the past now—no good getting miserable about it.'

Caroline wondered whether it had been Geoff or Elly who had ended the relationship, but she would question him no more. The thought of Geoff being hurt or unhappy was distressing to Caroline. She cared about him.

*   *   *

At first, there was nothing sexual about their relationship. It occurred to neither of them that there could be. As time passed, however, the occasional glance began to hold more than a friendly smile. Caroline noticed that Geoff would touch her shoulder as he passed her chair, which excited her and made her long to lay her hand on his to show that she was not offended but flattered.

She thought of Adam. He would have said, with all his youthful bluntness, that the chemistry was working. There was certainly a magnetism between them and if she was aware of it, Geoff must be too. The implicit nature of their mutual attraction made it all the more provocative and, at the same time, charming.

Whenever she thought in this way, Caroline would chide herself with a reminder that Geoff was ten years her junior—and that she was a married woman! With each and every pang of guilt, though, came the retort that Diane Tully was twenty years younger than Clive—and that he was a married man!

Occasionally, Caroline found herself behaving like a lovesick teenager. She would lie awake at night, wondering whether Geoff would ever make advances to her and what her reaction would be if he did. Perhaps she should make it known to him that her marriage was far from idyllic and that she suspected her husband of having an affair. Maybe Geoff would beg her to divorce Clive and start again with him . . . a new relationship . . . a new love.

Was this what she really wanted? A second chance!

It certainly seemed an attractive proposition.

Caroline's mind was in turmoil once more. This time, though, she felt that at least some kind of satisfactory conclusion might eventually come from the dilemma she now experienced.

If only Geoff would say something—tell her of his feelings. She was sure that he cared for her.

CHAPTER FOURTEEN

Geoff was a thinking man. Caroline had come to this conclusion after only a very short time in his presence. Like her, he was interested in nature conservation, but unlike her, he had joined several organizations so that he could take an active part in compensating for man's greed and stupidity.

It was refreshing for Caroline to be in the company of a man who cared little for possessions. His clothes were indicative of his way of life. He wore a clean shirt every day but the corners of the collar usually curled up just a little. The corduroy trousers, which he favoured, sometimes brown and sometimes grey, were slightly baggy at the knees and the behind but, like his well worn tweed jacket, they looked exceedingly comfortable. Caroline could imagine Geoff's home. It would not be smart and fashionable, like her own, but cosy and welcoming.

Whenever Caroline tried to analyze her feelings for Geoff she became troubled. It would be so easy for her to drift into a relationship with him. She knew that having an affair was a very real possibility for her, yet she was uncomfortable with the thought of committing adultery.

Her previous fears about divorcing Clive

were disappearing, now that she knew she need not be alone. Geoff was so easy-going and so delightful to be with, that the thought of a life with him evoked a picture of security and mutual trust, which tempted Caroline sorely to leave Clive.

It was her motives that caused her more anxiety than anything else. The question she found it impossible to answer was this: did she love Geoff or was she attracted to him because he was so unlike her erring, selfish husband? Was it his way of life she really yearned for? Maybe she was drawn to him because she felt flattered by his attentions . . . or worse still, because she saw Geoff as a way of gaining revenge over Clive and his Miss Tully. She was certainly attracted to Geoff, but could she truly say that she was in love with him? Why could she not bring herself to answer yes?

*   *   *

'I'm going to a Friends Of The Earth rally in a couple of weeks, Caroline,' Geoff announced one day as they were having their morning tea break. 'It's in North Wales—we're going to a wildlife sanctuary while we're there.'

'Sounds interesting.'

'Yes. I wondered . . . I thought that you might like to come?'

Caroline looked into Geoff's kind eyes.

'Oh, I see,' she murmured.

124

'We'd have to drive down on the Friday evening and we'd get back on Sunday night,' he explained. 'If you were interested . . . ?'

'Would we?'

'You know what I'm really asking you, don't you, Caroline?' Geoff whispered through a dry throat. He took her hand and kissed it gently.

'Yes, I know.' She bowed her head, blushing.

'I'm not in the habit of asking married women to come away with me for the weekend. It's just that . . . well . . . I feel very attracted to you . . . very much so . . . and I hoped . . .' Caroline's face lit up with a smile of warmth and tenderness. She gave Geoff's trembling hand a reassuring squeeze.

'I understand what you're saying, Geoff— and I would like to come with you—very much, but I need to think about it. Can I give you my answer tomorrow?'

'Of course.' Geoff smiled anxiously. 'I'm not very good at saying what I mean,' he continued. 'I don't want you to think that it's just sex though—it's much more than that. I think I'm in love with you, as a matter of fact.'

Caroline tried not to show just how elated she felt on hearing this enchanting declaration.

'You are?' she said softly.

'Your being married doesn't seem to have put up the usual stop signs for me.' Upon seeing her slightly quizzical expression, he expanded. 'Well, once I know a woman is already spoken for, I don't normally enter into anything but a good old platonic friendship with her. You're different, though, Caroline . . . whether you're married or not, my feelings for you have exceeded the boundaries of mere friendship. I want you more than I've ever wanted anyone in my life.'

'Even Elly?'

'Even Elly.'

Geoff gripped her hand tightly now; his eyes fixed on hers in a gaze that said more about desiring and yearning more than any words could do.

The door of Geoff's office opened and Mr. Allsworth walked in. Caroline's hand dropped onto the table and Geoff quickly snatched up a nearby letter to hide the truth of what had been happening.

'You'll let me know about that then, Caroline,' said Geoff loudly, as he turned to greet his uncle.

'Yes, I will,' she answered, trying to control her voice.

'Is it quite correct,' Mr. Allsworth asked in a precise manner, 'for a young man like yourself to call Mrs. Marshall by her Christian name?'

Caroline and Geoff glanced at each other. He smiled, but she suddenly felt very old.

*   *   *

That night, Caroline thought of little else but Geoff's invitation. She knew that he would not pressure her to go with him, but that meant that the weight of the decision was upon her alone.

If she did accompany him, she would become an adulteress. Is that what she wanted to be? Before long, her imagination aided her decision. Once again Caroline could see Clive and Diane Tully together. This time they were lying, naked, on a black satin sheet. Clive was groaning with absolute but forbidden ecstasy, whilst that whore dug her red, predatory talons into his muscular back. Again, Caroline was incensed. Yes! Yes, she would go with Geoff and, if he wanted her to, she would stay with him forever and leave her husband with the bimbo he so richly deserved!

Her decision made, Caroline tumbled slowly into sleep, anticipating the pleasure on Geoff's face when she gave him her answer.

* * *

'Oh, Caro,' Clive began, as they shared a hurried breakfast, 'I was going to tell you last night, but you were asleep by the time I remembered . . .'

'Remembered what?' she asked, only half listening to his words.

'You know we were going to David and Jenny's next week for dinner?'

'I vaguely remember something about it . . .'

'Well, scrub it. We won't be welcome.'

Caroline's interest was roused and she broke free from her dreamy haze.

'Why?' she inquired.

'Because they're getting a divorce.'

'What! David and Jenny! Why?'

'He's been having an affair with one of the clerks at the bank.'

Caroline could hardly believe what she was hearing.

'Who?' she asked, trying to appear unconcerned. 'Someone I know?'

'I don't think you know her . . . Diane Tully? You've probably heard her name, though. She's not been at the bank long. Very common—blonde, busty and not particularly bright.'

Caroline's mind swam as she tried to make sense of what Clive was telling her.

'Good Lord,' was all she could think of to say. There was a pause while Caroline calmed the shock that had caused her to feel momentarily sick. She attempted to order her thoughts. 'I always thought they were so happy,' she went on.

'To be honest, Caro, I thought you knew all about it,' Clive said, finishing his coffee.

'Me? How would I know about it?'

'You remember that night at the club a while back? You behaved very strangely when her name was mentioned. So I surmised that you knew all about it and were showing your disapproval.'

'No—I—I just wasn't feeling too well that night, now that I come to think of it.'

'I'm quite surprised you didn't know, actually. The damned fool didn't make much of a secret about it.'

'Really?'

'No, he told me about it ages ago—almost boasting, he was. I called him a bloody idiot to his face. Do you know, he even got me to take him to her house one night after squash so that his car wouldn't been seen in Poplar Close too often. He was in such a hurry to get to her that he left his sports bag in my boot, so I had to go chasing up her front drive with it like a damned servant. Not the way for a bank manager to behave in front of two members of his staff, even if it is outside banking hours. I told him that I wouldn't be taking him there any more, so he's either had to go in his own car or get some other mug to taxi him around. And as for her—she's been bragging to the other girls in the bank that she's having an affair with an older man, who was apparently showering her with expensive presents. It was bound to get back to Jenny sooner or later, the way they were carrying on.' There was another silence. 'Are you all right, Caro? You look rather pale this morning.'

'I'm fine.' She gave a weak smile. 'Bit of a headache, that's all.'

Clive left for work.

Caroline sat stunned and staring at nothing

in particular. She could not believe how utterly stupid she had been. All these months of anguish could have been avoided. Why had she not simply asked Clive what he had been doing in Poplar Close? He would have told her about David and Diane Tully there and then and that would have been an end to it. If only she had not been so afraid of being left alone that her only option had been to keep all that doubt and anger inside her. How could she have been such a coward, such a fool?

It was a wonder that Clive was not divorcing HER, after her behaviour over the summer months.

Caroline thought of Jenny. She pitied her. That night at the club, she had watched as David pretended to tell Clive where Diane lived. That deceit must have been for her benefit though, ironically, not for the reasons she had presumed because Clive had already taken him to the wretched girl's house. He had let Clive in on his secret, but he had tried to keep any hint of scandal away from her, in case she should tell Jenny. It was as though the males in this world would not betray each other's crimes, as though they had an unspoken code of conduct in such sordid matters, at least that is what David must have thought.

Caroline had been so certain, so very, very sure that Clive was being unfaithful to her. As she could be so wrong this time, she wondered if her suspicions when Adam was small were also groundless. Clive had probably been the faithful husband all along. Perhaps it was his immensely good looks which had helped to convince her that he was having affairs . . . maybe she had become obsessed with the fact that other women were attracted to him.

Caroline phoned the office. She told Mr. Allsworth that she had a blinding headache and would not be able to work that day.

She needed time to think. When Mrs. Curran arrived, Caroline explained that she was unwell and went upstairs to lie on her bed, leaving her help to work, as quietly as possible, downstairs.

As she lay there, Caroline's feelings of disbelief and anger at her own stupidity changed gradually to those of guilt and shame. She had thought of Clive, for some time now, as someone not to be trusted. In fact, she had been the one to fail in their marriage. He was innocent of the charges she had made in her mind.

Caroline's remorse was deepened by the knowledge that she had intended to go away with Geoff and commit adultery with him. Thank God she had found out the truth in time. She would tell Geoff that she could not go—it would not be easy after he had told her of his feelings. Clive must come first now though. She would try to make amends to him for her moody and sullen behaviour.

'Feeling better?' Mrs. Curran asked when Caroline came down just before lunch.

'I think so. Thanks.'

'Maybe this job's a bit too much for you, Mrs. Marshall. My sister, Olive, had to give up work just a few weeks ago—the doctor said . . .'

'No, it isn't the job, Mrs. Curran,' Caroline interrupted. 'More like too much cheese; it occasionally brings on a migraine.'

'Yes, well, don't you overdo it.'

Caroline smiled.

'I won't. I promise.'

After she had forced down a dish of soup, Caroline went next door to see Peggy. She missed their afternoon chats now that she was at work during the day and she knew that she would be welcome.

'Do you remember David and Jenny Hines?' Caroline asked, as she and Peggy sat down in the lounge.

'I think so—you've told me about them before, haven't you?'

'They're getting a divorce.'

'Really?'

'Yes. It's strange how things work out, isn't it?' Caroline said, almost wistfully. 'I always thought of Jenny as having everything just about right. You know—the woman who's got it all—the perfect life.'

'What happened? Another woman?'

'Yes. Poor Jenny . . . she must be

devastated.'

'Is he leaving her for his bit on the side, or did she do the sensible thing and throw him out?'

'I don't, know, Peggy. Clive says she's common—this girl—I can't see David settling down with someone like that.'

'They've got a little girl, too, haven't they?'

'Yes. It's bad for the children, when a marriage breaks up.'

'I wonder how many men take the same chance,' Peggy said thoughtfully.

'How do you mean?'

'Well, I wonder how many get away with it . . . have their bit of fun and don't get found out.' Peggy seemed agitated by the thought of such injustice.

'It happens quite a bit, I suppose . . . and women are often guilty too.'

'Oh, yes—we're not all saints by any means, are we?' The expression in Peggy's eyes intensified as she spoke. It was as if she was willing Caroline to understand some voiceless message, something which she could not bring herself to put into words.

Caroline turned away from her friend. She knew. Somehow, Peggy knew about her thwarted plans to commit adultery with Geoff. Caroline felt her face tingling hot and knew that she must look flushed. She shuffled about in her seat, briefly consumed by shame.

But this was ridiculous! Caroline rebuked

133

herself silently; she was being paranoid. How could Peggy possibly know what went on secretly in her own mind? Nobody could know. It wasn't possible by any stretch of the imagination. Whatever intimation or warning had appeared to be in her friend's eyes, it could not have been about that.

'I think I might give up my job,' stated Caroline, regaining her composure.

'But I thought you were enjoying it?'

'I was, but it's a bit much for me. Clive's often late for his clubs because his dinner isn't ready. And . . . well . . . I've tried being a working wife, but I don't feel it suits me. I think the novelty's worn off . . . so I'm handing in my notice.'

'Whatever you think is best, Caroline.'

*   *   *

Caroline took a letter of resignation to the office with her the following day.

Geoff looked hurt, as though he was not only disappointed, but wounded. It tore Caroline apart to see him like this, but she knew where her loyalties lay. She could not go on working in close proximity to him, not after what had almost happened between them.

She would miss her work terribly. It had been the most enjoyable interlude in her life for years. She would not only miss Geoff, but the elder Mr. Robertson too, and Mr.

Allsworth. She would miss the musty old house and the courtesy of her employers, but she had no choice.

Caroline was sure now that she had never loved Geoff. She had never stopped loving Clive.

CHAPTER FIFTEEN

The days that were spent working out her notice were uncomfortable for Caroline.

Geoff was unusually quiet and spoke only about work. She knew that she had made him unhappy and she was sorry for this, but she could say nothing to ease his misery. The guilt that she felt when in Geoff's presence was a minor perturbation, though, compared to the self-loathing she suffered when she was with Clive.

Caroline could tell no one of the shame that was eating away at her, allowing her no peace.

Though she had not actually been unfaithful to Clive, the fact that she had been planning to become Geoff's mistress seemed somehow more despicable than if she had made love to him in a moment of unexpected passion. The worst part of it all, though, was that she had believed Clive capable of infidelity.

*   *   *

On the night after she had finished work at Robertson & Allsworth's, Caroline and Clive made love. For her, it was perfect and beautiful. She felt that it was symbolic somehow, as though she were ending a period in her life during which she had been lost, a period when she had almost committed the most dreadful mistake imaginable—a turbulent time when she had known much misery.

As she lay there in the warmth of their bed, she tried to reason away her remorse, but she could not. Clive was a man who showed little emotion, except when he was making love. It was not his fault. It was the way he was made and that was that. He loved her though; she no longer needed reassurance about that. He was a faithful husband and a generous one. She did not deserve him.

There were bound to be differences in a marriage. Clive held certain views with which she disagreed, but she must be more flexible in her attitude and not condemn him in her heart or mind because of these differences. She would work hard at making him happy.

*   *   *

On the following Monday morning, Caroline got ready to visit her mother. She had been unable to see much of her mum while she had been working, and this had worried her.

It was a wet November morning and Caroline drove slowly to her mother's house. She would ask her to come and spend Christmas with them, as she did every year, and she would also try to delicately suggest that her mother should think about living somewhere where she could get proper care and attention at any hour of the day or night. The issue could be postponed no longer. Clive had probably been right when he said that it would not work if the old lady moved in with them permanently. Such arrangements often sound acceptable, even tempting, but in practice they are rarely successful.

Her mother was a reasonable woman; Caroline was sure that she would understand once she got used to the idea. It might even be a relief to her. She would always have company, after all, and be well looked after.

As Caroline turned the corner of her mother's road, her eyes widened and her heart froze in her chest. An ambulance stood, with its rear doors wide open and lights flashing, outside her mother's house.

'What's wrong? What's happened?' Caroline cried, as she got out of the car.

'Your mum's had another fall, love,' one of the neighbours answered, hurrying to Caroline's side.

'Oh my God! No!' Caroline raced to the front door of her mother's house as the paramedics carried the old lady out on a stretcher.

'Don't worry—she'll be all right,' called the neighbour. 'I tried to phone you, but you must have been on your way here.'

Caroline tried to offer words of comfort, as she kept pace with the moving stretcher, but the old lady's eyes were closed.

The neighbour guided a bewildered and frightened Caroline into the back of the ambulance and they both went with the unconscious woman to the hospital.

*　　*　　*

It seemed an age, waiting for the doctors to attend to her mother. Caroline's stomach churned over and over and quivered, cold as ice, while the kindly neighbour offered customary words of reassurance.

'She'll be fine, dear,' she whispered. 'Don't you worry . . . she's in the best place . . . these doctors will soon have her up and about.'

'I do hope so.'

'Would you like some hot, sweet tea? You've had a nasty shock yourself, you know.'

'No thanks. I couldn't possibly drink anything. I'd be sick.'

'Well . . . if you're sure.'

'How did it happen?' Caroline asked, still trying to compose herself and drive back the tears.

'Well, I went round the back way, like I always do,' the neighbour explained, 'to make sure your mum was all right—and I found her lying on the concrete path by the back step.'

'That's quite steep, isn't it?'

'It looked to me as if she'd been carrying her rubbish out to the dustbin; it was all over the path. I expect she either slipped on the wet concrete or missed her footing on the step.'

'Poor mum! If only I'd got there sooner, I could have put her damned rubbish out for her!' Caroline began to sob.

'Now, then, it's no good blaming yourself. These things happen and it's nobody's fault.'

'I should have got her to move ages ago. Clive said that I should talk to her about it back in the summer.'

'Move?'

'Yes, into an old people's home. I've been worried about her living alone for some time. I wanted her to move into our house, but Clive said it wouldn't be practical for anyone concerned, so it had to be a home.'

'I don't know that your mum would like the idea of that. She's quite an independent woman, isn't she?'

'That's why I've put the subject off for so long. I was going to talk to her about it today.'

Caroline held her breath as the waiting room door opened.

'Mrs. Marshall? I'm afraid your mother is seriously injured,' the doctor explained, in a compassionate yet business-like manner. 'She has a fractured right hip, a fractured right arm, and severe concussion. She hasn't regained consciousness yet, which is rather worrying.'

'Will she be all right? Can I see her?' Caroline asked, her voice dying in her throat.

'Just for a moment, but I want to do more tests as soon as possible.'

Caroline was shown into the room where her mother lay motionless. As she stared down at the ashen face, so very familiar and always so kind, she sobbed until she could not breathe. A nurse led her out. The neighbour telephoned for a taxi to take them both to the old lady's house, where Caroline could pick up her car. There was apparently nothing she could do whilst her mother was undergoing tests.

*   *   *

Peggy was walking back from the shops as Caroline arrived home. She saw her friend's obvious distress, and went to see if she could be of any help.

'I'll phone Clive for you, shall I?' Peggy suggested, once Caroline had told her of the morning's events.

'Yes . . . yes please.' Caroline sunk, trembling, onto the sofa and pulled her coat around her. She was cold and the disinfectant smell of the hospital lingered in her throat.

'He'll be home as soon as he can,' Peggy said, after her phone call to the bank. 'Now, let me get you something to eat and drink.'

'I couldn't keep it down . . . honestly, Peggy, I couldn't.'

'You must try and relax, Caroline. I know it's difficult, but do try to be calm.'

'Just as I thought things were . . .' Caroline began and then, remembering that her friend was in ignorance about her recent marital problems, she held back. 'Oh, take no notice of me, Peggy. I'm rambling, aren't I? I feel so drained.'

'Have a little sleep. You'll feel better if you do,' Peggy urged.

Caroline lay her head back and closed her swollen eyes. She was exhausted. Sleep washed over her in waves, but in between, there was a nebulous fear in her semi-slumbering mind, which would not subside.

*   *   *

Clive took Caroline back to the hospital directly he got home. She insisted that he should.

Her mother was still unconscious. The two of them stood staring helplessly at the old lady, Caroline willing her to open her eyes. She did not.

After only a short while, a nurse advised Clive to take Caroline back home. She promised to telephone if there was any change.

'I want to stay with her,' Caroline protested.

'There's nothing you can do, Caro,' Clive argued gently. 'She doesn't know we're here. It's much more sensible to get a good night's sleep in the comfort of your own home, then you'll feel fresher in the morning and you can come in again. She'll probably be awake by then.'

Clive was sympathetic and persuasive. Caroline acquiesced.

Two Valium ensured that she slept soundly all that night.

*   *   *

The following morning, Caroline phoned the hospital at eight o'clock. Her mother had developed pneumonia.

As Caroline and Clive sat silently by her bed, later that morning, the old lady died without having regained consciousness.

Caroline was inconsolable.

CHAPTER SIXTEEN

The sense of loss Caroline felt after the death of her mother was as great a sorrow as she had ever known.

When she looked back over the years, to any time in her life, her mother had always been there, cheerful and dependable and strong. To think that she had gone forever, and with so little warning, was at first, unbelievable and then unacceptable. Caroline cried until she thought there could be no more grief left in her, but still the sadness welled up and took hold of her heart. The tears would not stop.

The practical business of death had to be dealt with. Caroline relied on Clive a great deal at this time. He sent letters informing the family of the bereavement, and arranged the funeral. It occurred to Caroline more than once, that if she had been alone, she could not have coped.

Clive was her strength.

At first, she did not allow herself to even consider that her mother's death could have been prevented. It was simply too painful. After a few days, though, she could ignore her true feelings no longer.

If only she had persuaded her mum to move into a home. Why had she not even talked to her about it? Why had she not made sure that her mother was properly looked after? Such questions passed through Caroline's mind constantly; once again she was crushed by self-reproach.

She never once blamed Clive for refusing her mother a home, not any more. No, she was still coming to terms with her cruel and groundless accusations against him. It seemed appropriate, therefore, that she should carry the entire burden of guilt concerning her mother. It was as though she was being punished for her wicked suspicions of Clive, and accepting this punishment gave her a strange satisfaction. There was a sense of justice about it all.

*   *   *

The day of the funeral was also the day on which Caroline and Clive had been due to fly off for their holiday in Venice. After the old lady's death, they had decided that they would not cancel their trip, but postpone it until the following spring. Clive took care of altering the arrangements.

As the relatives and friends arrived at the crematorium, Caroline tried to present the image of a grieving, but composed daughter. She mingled with aunts and uncles that she had not seen for years, determined not to break down in the midst of this sombre gathering.

The day was bright, but blustery, and everyone had wrapped up against the cold November wind.

Caroline looked around at the assembled mourners, and wished that she could be someone else.

In the chapel, she could conceal her inflamed emotions no longer. As the curtains closed, in front of the coffin, she cried aloud and called for her mother. Clive had to restrain her. Adam looked horrified.

Caroline suddenly felt terribly alone. Though she could feel Clive's arms around her shoulders, it was only her sobs that echoed around the stone walls of the chapel. She wiped her eyes and looked around her. No one else was crying. Even Adam showed no sign of real sorrow.

Caroline knew that nobody else was grieving as she was.

The winter wind was cool and refreshing on her burning face, as she walked between Clive and Adam into the fresh air. She took deep breaths and gradually became calmer—or at least more controlled.

Her relatives followed her out of the chapel. Caroline had an urge to face them and scream out:

'Why aren't you crying? My mother is dead! Why don't you cry, damn you!' But she had neither the energy nor the courage.

*　　　*　　　*

When they got back to the house, Peggy had just finished preparing a cold buffet in the lounge.

'Thanks,' Caroline whispered, taking her

friend's hand. 'You've been such a help, Peggy. I don't know what I would have done . . .'

'Don't be silly, Caroline,' Peggy interrupted. 'It's nothing. I'll disappear now; you know where I am if you need me again.'

Caroline watched as Peggy slipped quietly out of the back door. She was a true friend.

The guests hovered in small groups and spoke in suitably low tones. Everyone pecked at the food, but nobody wanted to be seen eating heartily.

'Well, you'll be able to get back to normal once today's over,' Caroline's Aunt Jessie murmured in her ear.

'Yes,' Caroline replied, not quite sure how she should answer, and not feeling inclined to indulge in small talk with anyone.

'It's always a good thing to get this sort of do over and done with,' Aunt Jessie went on, 'Nothing to run after are they . . . funerals?'

'No . . . no, they're not.' Caroline slowly shook her bowed head.

'You young folk have got your lives to get on with. You don't want to be harping on death at your age. You'll be old soon enough . . . like me!' Aunt Jessie giggled and wandered off, with a large sherry in her hand.

The relatives began to drift away. Many of them had long journeys to make; Caroline's mother had been originally from the north of England. It was a relief to see them go. Her house being once more her own, Caroline

146

found solace in clearing up and loading her dishwasher. Such familiar actions brought a feeling of security, and Caroline needed that so much at this unhappy time, when she had been starkly reminded of her own mortality.

Adam caught the last train back to Cambridge; he would be home again for Christmas.

*　　*　　*

'I got the feeling that no one else really cared,' Caroline explained to Peggy the following morning.

'I'm sure they did!'

'I know Clive and Adam did. They're very similar, you know, and neither one of them shows his feelings very much. Apart from them, though, it seemed that everyone else had come because it would be impolite not to, and that the sooner it was all over and mum forgotten, the better!'

'You only felt like that because you were upset, Caroline,' Peggy said reassuringly.

'Perhaps. But I'm not convinced. It was as if the whole business was a nuisance . . . as though it had stopped everyone getting on with their stupid, boring lives . . . an annoying interruption to most of those so-called mourners . . . that's all it was.'

*　　*　　*

147

The following weeks were difficult beyond belief. Caroline tried desperately to shelve her feelings of guilt about the way her mother's life had ended. She knew, however, that she could have done more to make the old lady happier and, what was harder to come to terms with, was the knowledge that if she had not been living alone, her mother would still have been alive.

To blame herself was a futile act. Nothing could undo what had happened. Caroline did blame herself, though, and the agony she suffered was made worse because she grieved in isolation. Clive would be highly irritated if she told him how she felt; he would say that she was over-reacting. So she confided in no one.

*   *   *

Christmas that year was a subdued affair in the Marshall household. Adam came home and the usual traditions were upheld, but the levity was missing.

Caroline just wanted it all to be over. She wished that time would pass and, being the supposedly great healer, do its work.

*   *   *

Half way through January, Adam returned to

Cambridge. Caroline did not ask if he had seen Christine and he offered no information on the subject.

The day after Adam left, Caroline sat browsing through the local newspaper when a familiar face smiled at her from its pages.

'Mr. Geoffrey Robertson, a solicitor from the firm of Robertson and Allsworth,' she read aloud, 'married Miss Kathleen Houghton at St. Luke's Church, on Saturday, the fourteenth of January.'

The picture showed a happy bride and groom.

'You're a lucky girl, Miss Kathleen Houghton—er—Mrs. Robertson,' Caroline whispered, feeling, just for a moment, deeply jealous.

*   *   *

'Let's go to London next week, Caroline,' Peggy suggested one afternoon. 'I still haven't had my day roaming around the galleries and it's so much more enjoyable if there are two of you. We can treat ourselves to lunch, too— make a real day of it. What do you say?'

'Oh, yes, please, Peggy! Let's go! Get rid of the January blues—for a while at least.'

'What about next Saturday, then? Steven can supervise the twins—he won't mind.'

'Ok, it's a date. It'll be something to look forward to. I haven't been out for ages.'

*　　*　　*

That night, as she tried to sleep, Caroline thought of Geoff. She remembered how they used to laugh together, and she saw again his warm, blue eyes looking at her . . . wanting her.

'I love you Clive,' she whispered.

He was asleep.

CHAPTER SEVENTEEN

The day in London started well. It was cold, but sunny and invigorating. Caroline and Peggy caught the early train and, by eleven o'clock, they were enjoying morning coffee in the big city.

'How about the Tate first?' Peggy suggested.

'Yes, sounds fine.'

'I think it's best if we get a taxi—what do you think?'

'Absolutely. I hate the tube.'

Caroline took some aspirin from her bag.

'Not feeling too good?' Peggy asked.

'Just a bit of a headache; it'll pass.'

The two friends took a taxi to the Tate Gallery, and sauntered among the works of art.

Caroline could see that Peggy was enchanted by what she saw so she tried to hide the fact that her headache was growing worse. As she looked at the paintings, vivid, flashing lights began to impair her vision, and she knew that a migraine was developing. By the time they left the gallery, she felt terribly sick.

'Where shall we go for lunch?' Peggy enthused.

'It's no good, Peggy. I've been trying to ignore it, but I've got a dreadful migraine.'

'I thought you weren't yourself. Come on, we'll go home—we can always come back another time.'

'You carry on, Peggy. You've wanted to do this for so long. I'll get the next train home. I'll be fine. I just have to lie down in a dark room for a while—there's nothing else for it.'

'I'm coming with you.'

'No. I don't want to spoil your day. Honestly, I'll be all right on my own.'

'Caroline—I'm coming with you, and that's that! We can always come back another day to finish our tour of the galleries.'

Caroline had not the strength to argue, and she was glad of the company. They took a taxi to the station. The noise of the crowded, bustling streets did not improve Caroline's condition. Her head was racked with pain by the time their train pulled out of the station, and she dared not eat or drink because of the nausea she felt. She sat with her eyes closed and longed to be home. Peggy knew that conversation would be unwise, so she stared out at the countryside as the train speedily left the metropolis behind.

*   *   *

After what seemed like an age the two women arrived home, Peggy having driven from the station.

'Thank God,' Caroline mumbled. 'I'm so sorry to have spoilt your day for you, Peggy.'

'Don't give it another thought. We'll make up for it soon.'

'I've just got to get to bed.'

'I know. In you go—I'll see you later.'

Caroline gently closed the front door behind her. The silence was a relief. She walked out of her shoes and began to climb the stairs, holding on to the banisters for support. Clive, she knew, would be out playing golf. He would find out she was back soon enough.

She absently pushed open the bedroom door. The sight that met her unsuspecting and throbbing eyes caused her to stagger, almost fainting, against the wall.

There, lying naked and asleep in each other's arms, were Clive and June—her hairdresser!

Caroline stood for a moment, her eyes held by this devastating scene. She seemed fixed to the spot on which she stood. Then, as though he was suddenly aware of her presence, Clive

152

turned his head and opened his heavy eyes.

'Oh my God,' he said quietly.

June woke on hearing his words. She stared icily at Caroline, but said nothing.

Not knowing what else to do, but instinctively wanting to distance herself from such an odious spectacle, Caroline slammed the bedroom door and ran, unsteady on her feet, down the stairs and out of the house. She was almost blind now with the pain in her head, and, as she reached Peggy's house, she began to cry hysterically.

'Caroline! Whatever's wrong?' gasped a shocked Peggy, as Caroline stumbled in through her back door.

'Cli . . . Clive,' she sobbed.

'What's happened to him?' Peggy had visions of Clive lying dead in a pool of blood.

Caroline slumped down in a chair.

'Oh God!' she cried.

'Caroline, what's happened?' Peggy pleaded, becoming more alarmed with every second that passed.

'He . . . he's . . . I . . . found . . . found him . . .' She seemed incapable of finding enough breath in her lungs to say what she had witnessed. '. . . June . . . I found him . . . in bed . . . with . . . with . . . my hairdresser . . .' Fury and desolation united in her eyes and her voice as she shouted out this revelation, her hand pointing wildly in the direction of her bedroom.

Peggy sighed. She held Caroline's head against her body and stroked her hair gently, as a mother comforts her fretting offspring.

'Poor love,' she whispered.

The fact that she had told someone brought a certain kind of relief to Caroline. She felt the tension drain from her muscles and she cried until she could cry no more.

'I'll make you some tea,' Peggy said softly.

'What can I do?' Caroline implored, a child-like bewilderment etched on her face.

'Nothing at this moment,' Peggy replied. 'Just sit quietly and I'll get you a cup of tea.'

There was silence for a few minutes. Caroline tried to untangle her rampaging thoughts. She struggled to find logic in all of this.

'He must have gone for a haircut this morning and had a brainstorm or something,' she reasoned. 'I'll bet he asked her to come round on the spur of the moment . . . or maybe she was the one to make the move! . . . I know she fancied him; she's often told me that she thought he was good-looking. Yes . . . yes, she'd be the one to do the propositioning, the bitch!'

'Look . . . you've got to know,' Peggy blurted, 'Clive and June have been having an affair for ages—it must be a couple of years now, I think. I can't see you deceived like this any longer.'

Caroline's already over-emotional state

became suddenly more volatile as she attempted to take in what Peggy had just said.

'I wanted to tell you before,' her friend explained gently.

'Then why the hell didn't you?!' Caroline yelled, anger flashing in her eyes.

'Steven and I discussed it and we decided that it would be best to keep out of it. There was always the chance that Clive would drop her. It could have been a passing fling, and you need never have known. It isn't an easy thing to tell someone, Caroline. We could have been breaking up your marriage.'

'It's Clive that's broken up our marriage!'

'I tried to tell you, Caroline—I really did—when you found out about David Hines and his bank clerk, but I just couldn't bring myself to do it.'

Caroline realized, now, what she had seen in Peggy's eyes on that day.

'Well, I wish you had done!'

'Don't be angry with me, Caroline. Please!'

'What do you expect? You're supposed to be my best friend and yet you watched me being deceived like this! And for a couple of years?!'

'I didn't know what to do for the best.'

'So you let him—and her—make an absolute fool of me! I'll bet she was laughing her head off whenever she was doing my hair!'

'Caroline . . . don't.'

'And I'll bet you had a good laugh, too—you

155

and Steven! I expect the whole bloody world knew about this!'

'Don't be so ridiculous, Caroline!'

Caroline let out a snort of derision. 'Yes, I am pretty ridiculous, aren't I?'

'Listen . . .'

'NO! No, I won't listen! And I won't forgive you for your part in all of this, either!'

'My part?'

'Yes . . . yes! I could have started a new life with another man—a man I thought a great deal of, a man who loved me—but I didn't, because of that rat I call my husband, because of Clive bloody Marshall and my stupid loyalty to him! And now it's too late . . . because Geoff's married to someone else! If only you'd told me! And you have the bare-faced audacity to call yourself a friend?'

'I'm so sorry, Caroline. I had no idea.'

'It's no bloody good being sorry, is it?! I thought I could trust you! You've ruined everything for me—almost as much as Clive has! Keep out of my life now . . . for the sake of my sanity . . . just stay away from me!'

Caroline wandered back home, dazed and in shock. She was sure that June would have gone by now and she was right. Clive sat in the lounge drinking a large whisky.

'Caro,' he said as she entered, 'don't get this out of proportion, please.'

She stared at him, her eyes alive with incredulity and hatred.

'What?' she barked.

'I've told June that it's all over,' he declared. 'I'm not seeing her any more.' No shame was discernable in Clive's face.

'I see.' Caroline replied, with as much composure as she could muster. 'And I'm supposed to pretend that your affair with her—an affair that's apparently been going on for quite some time—never happened? Is that right?'

'Er . . . no. I don't mean that exactly. But honestly, Caro, nearly every married man I know has had . . .'

'A bit on the side?' Caroline interrupted.

'Well . . . yes.'

'And that makes it all right, does it?'

'Look, Caro . . .'

'No, Clive! I won't!'

Caroline took a large crystal rose bowl, which Clive had won at a golf tournament, from its position of pride on a specially erected shelf. She held it high up in the air and then smashed it into a million sparkling splinters at his feet. She wished that she had the courage to throw it at his head.

Clive winced and then raised his eyebrows passively. Yes, even in this situation he would be thinking that she was over-reacting.

Slowly, Caroline went upstairs and locked herself in the spare bedroom. She could not bear to go into her own room—their room—where she had witnessed her husband and his

157

mistress lying so peacefully in each other's arms, so natural together.

Her headache seemed easier now, other matters having over-ridden its importance. She lay on the bed and closed her eyes. She felt utterly exhausted.

*   *   *

As she lay there, still bruised from her migraine, and unable to bear the mental anguish which had descended upon her, Caroline's thoughts darted haphazardly from one ghastly event to the next.

She thought of Clive and June: she could not erase the sight of them from her mind's eye. It made her feel sick—it made her feel viscous. Then dear Geoff would enter her thoughts, gently and lovingly, but he was married now—it was all too late—how cruel.

Her row with Peggy had left her hurt and distressed, too. She felt a fool, on top of everything else. A fool for not realizing what had been happening. The fact that Peggy had not told her the truth was painful, but the row between them—the first ever—meant that she had lost her best friend.

Caroline wished so very much that she could confide in her mother about all that had happened. She missed the old lady dreadfully. There was still so much guilt too . . . not about Clive, though, not now. The only judgement she had made in error about him was the identity of his mistress. Caroline remembered the dreadful remorse she had suffered when she had believed him to be innocent. What a stupid, gullible idiot she had been! And to think that Clive had called David Hines 'a damned fool'! She realized now that Clive thought him a fool, not because of the affair with the Diane Tully, but because he had been caught.

Then there was June. June who had always been so friendly, so kind, the cow! How she must have been laughing at her! They probably talked about her, June and Clive, when they were alone together.

Even Adam and Christine came repeatedly back to her teeming consciousness. She wondered how Christine had coped with the abortion and if she had tried to see Adam again. Poor, dear Christine.

Caroline opened her eyes and sat up. The hatred she felt for June was fierce; she had never known such acute misery. How would she cope? There was no one she could turn to now—no one.

As her thoughts continued to bludgeon frantically through the disasters that had befallen her during the last year, Caroline felt that she was losing her mind. There was only turmoil; nothing made sense. She felt so alone, though, so bereft of all friends and so utterly unhappy that the thought of losing her sanity, her awareness of reality, was somehow pleasing to her.

CHAPTER EIGHTEEN

Caroline spent that night in the spare bedroom. Clive did not attempt to persuade her to do otherwise. She slept in spasms, a troubled uneasy sleep, and in between she turned this way and that, her confused mind allowing her no respite from her misery.

The following day being Sunday meant that she and Clive would be unable to avoid each other.

When she woke, Caroline decided that a bath might be therapeutic. She wanted to cleanse her body. She felt the need to rid herself of London, of her migraine . . . of everything that had occurred on the previous day.

Though she emerged from the warm, scented water feeling outwardly refreshed, her heart and her thoughts were, predictably, as heavy as before.

'Feeling better?' Clive asked as Caroline entered the kitchen.

'Not really,' she snapped.

'Coffee?'

'Yes.' Caroline sat down opposite Clive but her eyes avoided his.

'We need to clear the air, Caro,' he said gently. 'It's no good living with this atmosphere between us—we must talk.'

'Must we?'

'Yes. I'm sorry . . . O.K.? Is that what you want to hear? I was wrong.'

Clive appeared to be genuine in his desire to placate Caroline, but she knew he was lying. His words were hollow with no hint of remorse.

'And I'm supposed to accept that, am I? You've apologized and so we forget all about your affair—your prolonged affair—with a woman I knew well and even classed as a friend. We just pretend it never happened, do we, Clive?' Caroline's voice was trenchant and her face was flushed.

'There's no point in dwelling on it, Caro.'

'Isn't there?'

'No. I've told June that I don't want to continue seeing her. It's all over!'

'Just like that? It sounds so simple. I wonder why you didn't drop her before.' Caroline smiled sarcastically. 'All the time the deceit was working, all the time you could enjoy your bit of illicit sex and keep all your home comforts, too, you were happy to do so. Once the missus found out, though, then a quick choice had to be made, and it was over in a flash.'

'Caro . . .'

'Listen!' she screamed petulantly, before

calming herself and continuing with as much control as was possible in her present state. 'So . . . you chose to stay with me. I assume that I'm supposed to be relieved about that—grateful even—well I'm not! I'm not! Do you hear me? If you stay with me, we keep this house, we continue to be a respectable married couple with all our possessions intact. There won't be a scandal to interfere with your career—it's difficult to become a bank inspector with a messy divorce behind you, isn't it? June might talk, of course, but that's all right. The chaps at the bank will just snigger about it—"Bit of a lad, is old Clive!"—that's the kind of thing they'll say. Just as long as there's no divorce, as long as we are ostensibly the ideal couple and we can continue to entertain all those ghastly bank officials, your career will be unaffected! And that's what made you choose me, Clive! I don't think anything as corny and emotional as love even entered your head, did it?'

'Of course I love you, Caro,' Clive whispered, his quietness contrasting strongly with Caroline's excitable and unsteady voice.

'Really? That's why you found it necessary to have an affair, is it? Because you love me?'

'I told you, Caro, most married men . . .'

'Oh, no, Clive! Don't come that one again—"we're all in it so it's perfectly acceptable"—no way! Firstly, not all men are unfaithful to their wives. And, anyway, I'm not interested in what

162

your trendy friends get up to or how they boast about their conquests! You're my husband—you're the only one that matters to me! I don't care if every bloody male in the universe has a bit on the side! It's only you that I'm interested in!'

'Calm down, Caro. Please.'

'Oh, yes—I'm supposed to be grateful that you've chosen me, and I've got to pretend that nothing ever happened, haven't I? I'd forgotten for a moment what is expected of me!'

'I don't expect you to pretend it never happened, Caro!' Clive still tried to reason with her. 'The affair is over, though, and the sooner we can think of it as a thing in the past—a mistake, if you like—the sooner we can rebuild our relationship. A lot of couples say that their marriage has been greatly improved by such a crisis.'

'Do they? Do they really?'

'Yes. We can work together at pleasing each other, really try to build up a good partnership—better than before.'

'And suppose I don't want to build up "a good partnership"? Suppose I no longer want to be married to you?' Caroline spoke strongly and calmly now.

Clive's eyes mirrored the shock he felt at his wife's words.

'What?' he murmured after a moment of silence.

'Did that not occur to you?' Caroline found satisfaction at Clive's stunned expression. 'Did you never consider the possibility that I might not want you in my life any more?'

'Well . . .'

'No, Jenny Hines can divorce David, but that's her. She's an independent woman. She can cope with or without a man at her side. Caro would never give Clive his marching orders, would she? Not poor little dependent Caro! She'd never survive on her own! And what about the lovely house, and the lovely swimming pool that only needs decorating, and the bloody landscaped garden? She'd never give all that up because her husband did the dirty on her!'

'Caro!'

'Well, she just might not want it all, Clive! And she might not want you!'

'We can be happy again,' Clive insisted.

'Not if I want a divorce, we can't!'

'Is that what you want?'

'I might! Give me a couple of days to think it over and I'll get back to you!'

Caroline sauntered to the lounge and lay down on the sofa. She knew that she had at least given Clive something to think about. His presumption that she would stay with him had acted as a kind of challenge to her; the arrogance of the man was beyond belief.

'Caro . . .' Clive began, joining her in the lounge.

'I don't feel like cooking Sunday lunch,' she interrupted, 'so I'm not going to. I don't want to talk any more, either. I just want to think things over quietly.'

Caroline closed her eyes, and Clive cooked lunch.

* * *

The remainder of the day was spent in near silence and, not for the first time, Caroline felt relief when Clive left for work the following morning.

Mrs. Curran arrived and began her usual chores. She could see that her employer was not in a talkative mood so she busied herself quietly.

Doing all her own housework again would not come easy, Caroline thought, as she watched her help attack the oven, which had been left in a somewhat greasy state after Clive's confrontation with the roast lamb. She certainly would not be able to afford a cleaner herself if she divorced him. The house would probably be sold, so she would have to find a flat—and a job. If only she had not left Robertson & Allsworth's. If only she had gone with Geoff! Why had her life become a painful torrent of regret?

Caroline went upstairs. She sat on the bed in the spare room, where she had spent another restless night and where she intended to spend every night, until she had decided what she was going to do.

It was a difficult thing to admit to herself, but Caroline had begun to consider the inconvenience of a divorce. She was thinking of possessions and practicalities—just as she had accused Clive of doing.

The truth was that she still felt that old panic at the thought of coping on her own. She would keep her fears to herself, though. It could be the making of her, to live alone and make her own way in the world. She had been happy at Robertson & Allsworth's—why should she not find another job she enjoyed? Another Geoff, though, was too much to hope for.

Making the break was the hard part . . . taking the chance. It was so tempting to stay with Clive because of the sheer convenience and familiarity of it.

Then Caroline thought of June. Anger governed her reasoning once more. How could she even consider staying with a man who had deceived her so cruelly?

How she wished that she was strong enough to go to June and tell her exactly what she thought of her! Perhaps throw something at her! Or punch her in her lying, painted mouth! The fury was there, tearing at her very soul, as the lion tears at its quarry. How could she contain such savage hatred? Why could she not confront the other woman? She had every

166

right to! She was the innocent and injured party; June was the adulteress. Why had she not the strength to face the whore? She longed to attack her physically, to leave her scarred and ugly, but she knew that she would simply keep away from her.

The same weakness, which prevented her from standing up to June, also tempted her to opt for the financial comfort and security of a home with Clive. Caroline hated herself. She loathed her lack of fortitude and her pathetic, dithering indecisiveness.

*   *   *

It was beginning to snow. The sky had been darkening all morning and the white breaths of passers-by hung icily on the air.

Caroline stood close to the window; she watched as the soft and fragile flakes fell past her. Some of them landed on the glass and melted, while others were determined to get to the ground. It was soothing to stare at the gentle, tumbling movement of the snowflakes. Gradually, the road and pavements were turning white.

Caroline smiled. The world and all its filth were being hidden . . . disguised by a dazzling, blinding purity.

CHAPTER NINETEEN

That night, Caroline slept more soundly than she had done since her fateful day in London. The only reason for her peaceful, if unnatural, slumber being the three tranquilizers that she had taken before going to bed.

She did not hear Clive leave for work and she was pleased to have the house to herself when she finally woke.

As she made some coffee, still drowsy and slightly numbed from the Valium, Caroline saw Peggy wave from her kitchen window. She turned quickly away, not wishing to meet her friend's apprehensive gaze. She had acted on impulse and immediately afterwards felt foolish, even childish, because she had not acknowledged Peggy's familiar, if anxious, smile.

Caroline had not forgiven Peggy for failing to tell her of Clive's affair, but she knew that her friend had acted in what she had thought to be the kindest way. Peggy would never do anything to hurt her intentionally. Caroline decided that she would go next door and make her peace later that day. In her anger she had said some dreadful things to Peggy for which she would apologize. She also intended to explain that she realized how difficult Peggy and Steven's position must have been. After all, if she ever needed a good friend, it was now . . . she needed Peggy.

After breakfast Caroline bathed and dressed. The tranquilizers were finally wearing off and she felt wide wake, exposed to reality once more.

The snow was two or three inches deep, but the morning sky was clear and a slow thaw had begun. Caroline wished that the glistening white covering would remain forever. It reminded her of icing sugar on a cake and even Clive's garden looked beautiful when robed in this delicate winter raiment.

The morning drifted past, almost unnoticed by Caroline, who was once again buried deep in the midst of perplexity.

Though Clive had given her the time she had requested to deliberate on the future (and had not yet asked her what her decision was to be) she knew that he would not remain silent on the subject for very much longer.

Part of her tried desperately to summon the strength to tell him that she was about to consult her solicitors and sue for divorce. Yet, at the same time, the side of her character that she loathed—that cowardly and feeble part of her nature—urged her to stay put and count her blessings. Millions of other women had managed to forgive such an affair, even if to forget proved impossible. Time would gradually ease the pain and erase that picture of her husband and his harlot, which still succeeded in dominating her thoughts.

If she did divorce him, Caroline was certain that she would be the one to suffer the most from the split. She would be alone and struggling financially, whereas Clive would soon find another wife—maybe even June—and still have his lucrative position at the bank, even if promotion would be difficult for him to achieve. He would substitute another woman in her place, and life for him would go on as usual.

Quite suddenly, Caroline knew that she must stay with Clive. If she did not, she might be giving him to June. And she refused to take that chance—why should that bitch have him? Why should she allow June to take over her husband and her lifestyle, while she lived a lonely—and unhappy—one? Who was she trying to punish, for God's sake?

She no longer loved Clive. The moment she had pushed open that bedroom door and seen him with his mistress was the instant she had stopped loving him. But perhaps some of the old affection would return in time. If it did not, then she would at least have the satisfaction of knowing that June could not have him. She would play the part of the contented wife and be consoled by the fact that millions of other women were doing the same.

Caroline poured herself a glass of wine to celebrate her decision.

She resolved that if life with Clive became

too unbearable, she would divorce him at a later date. For now, though, she would take the most convenient option and agree to the lesser of two evils. Her principles would have to be shelved, and her chronic indignation at Clive's treatment of her left largely unappeased.

Once again, the wrong side of her being had triumphed, but she would try to ignore that fact.

The wine made Caroline feel drowsy and she dozed by the fire for an hour or so. When she awoke, she decided that it was time to go next door and apologize to Peggy for the unfair attack she had launched on her. It was never easy to make a move towards reconciliation after such a blazing row, but she knew that Peggy would understand how distressed she had been and she was cheered by the thought that they would soon be enjoying their afternoon cups of tea again, like they used to.

CHAPTER TWENTY

The snow was melting fast as Caroline went round to Peggy's back door.

A dirty, grey wetness was rapidly replacing the crisp whiteness, and Caroline was sad to see it. The world was showing her true colours again.

'Peggy!' she called, as she knocked and pushed open the door. 'Peggy! It's me—Caroline!'

The house was silent. It was not like Peggy to leave her back door unlocked while she went out. Maybe she, too, had been lulled off to sleep by a warm fire.

Caroline quietly opened the door of the lounge. Peggy was not there, and the fire was out. On the coffee table lay a folded piece of paper, propped up against an ashtray. Perhaps she had gone off to the boys' school, or something of the kind, and left a note. It all seemed rather odd, and, as the letter was not sealed in an envelope, Caroline thought that it could not be private, so she picked up the paper and read:

Dear Steven,

I found a lump in my other breast this morning and after much agonizing, I decided that I could not face all that awful business over again. I'm sorry, but I'm a coward. It seemed so unfair to put you and the twins through the misery of watching me die slowly of a disease that I do not think I could conquer.

Please, Steven, find yourself another wife. I don't want you to be alone.

I love you,

Peg.

X

'Peggy!' Caroline screamed, as the true horror of what she had read sunk into her tortured mind. 'Peggy!' She ran up the stairs, tripping in her panic, her heart pounding so hard and fast that it hurt inside her chest.

As she opened the door of Peggy and Steven's bedroom, Caroline halted suddenly, terrified at the thought of what she might find. She took a deep breath and entered; she knew that she must.

Peggy lay seemingly unconscious on the bed. Two empty pill bottles stood, as though gloating, on the bedside table. Caroline moved towards her friend. She reached out, with fingers that trembled wildly, and touched Peggy's hand . . . it was warm! A fleeting relief passed over her.

Caroline ran downstairs and grabbed the receiver from the phone in the hall. Her fingers were ungovernable and it seemed an age before she managed to dial 999. She summoned an ambulance and ran back upstairs to Peggy.

For a moment, she stood staring at the motionless form of her best friend.

There was no time now to feel regret about their row, or guilt because of the way she had turned her back on Peggy that morning. No, she must act—she must try to help.

What should she do, though? Keep her warm . . . yes! Caroline grabbed the nearby duvet and covered her friend gently. What else? She should try to wake her . . . yes, that was it! Frantically, Caroline patted Peggy's pallid face, and tried to call her name. Her own mouth was so dry now, however, that she could make no sound. She coughed and dragged her tongue around her teeth in an attempt to moisten her throat; a broken and strained attempt at speech was the most she could produce. There was no response. She took the hands, which lay limply on the bed, and rubbed them together for what seemed like hours. What else should she do? Caroline's thoughts were desperately confused. Make her sick . . . yes, she should try to make her sick . . . fingers down the throat . . . that would work!

Just as she was about to lift Peggy's head from the pillow she heard sirens heralding the arrival of the ambulance.

'Thank God!' she gasped, as she ran downstairs to open the front door.

The ambulance men were soon with Peggy, and Caroline stood back as they carried her friend, on a stretcher, down the stairs. She went in the ambulance, talking to Peggy all the time and rubbing her hands and face in a fevered attempt to rouse her. She had no success.

The ambulance men said little, but their faces were grave.

'Why aren't you doing anything?' she

demanded of them. 'Can't you give her oxygen or something? She's going to be all right, isn't she?'

'Let's just get her to the hospital,' came the solemn reply.

Peggy's head rolled from side to side as the ambulance rushed around the wet streets. The skin around her closed eyes was dark, and her lips were almost white.

'Peggy!' Caroline pleaded in a frenzy of panic. 'Wake up, Peggy! Please!'

'Settle down, love,' one of the paramedics whispered, putting his hand on Caroline's shoulder. 'She can't hear you.'

Once in the waiting room at the hospital, Caroline sat dazed and frightened.

A nurse asked her where Peggy's family could be contacted. Caroline could not think where Steven worked; she felt stupid, but then it came to her. She was offered a cup of tea, but she could only swallow a little.

Sitting there, in the hospital, Caroline was reminded of her mother's accident—and of her death. It could not happen to Peggy, though, not like this . . . not like this!

'Please, God, make Peggy live,' Caroline whispered into her tightly clasped hands. 'Please, God, make her be all right.'

Steven arrived after only a very few minutes. Caroline saw the doctor take him into another room.

'I'm afraid your friend is dead,' a voice said

gently. Caroline looked up to see the face of a young nurse.

'No,' she mumbled, in a very small and tight voice, shaking her head in numb disbelief.

'I'm afraid she was dead on arrival at the hospital. There was nothing we could do.'

For several minutes, Caroline sobbed uncontrollably. The nurse's words of comfort afforded her none.

Steven entered, red-eyed, from the other room. Caroline rushed to his side.

'I tried, Steven,' she cried. 'I did everything I could think of, but I think she must have been d . . . already gone . . . when I found her.' Caroline could not bring herself to say that word . . . not when speaking of Peggy. 'The ambulance men seemed to know . . . they didn't do anything to her . . . I should have guessed . . .'

'I'll drive you home, Caroline,' Steven said with quiet gravity. 'There's nothing we can do here. I don't want to see her. Not yet, anyway.'

'She left a note, Steven,' Caroline explained as they drove through the town. 'She'd found another lump.'

'Poor Peg,' he said. It was as if he was talking from habit . . . mechanically. He was clearly in shock. 'Poor Peg,' he repeated.

'Do you want to be alone?' Caroline asked, once they had arrived back home. 'You can come in with Clive and me, if you don't.'

'No, no . . . I've got to talk to the twins . . .'

Steven replied. 'I don't know how I can tell them, but I've got to find a way. I must be there when they get home.'

Caroline could imagine Steven reading Peggy's note. She thought of him alone and weeping; there seemed nothing at all that she could do.

Clive was not home yet: it was still only half past three. It seemed much later than that.

As she turned on the fire and sat by its warm, amber glow, Caroline shed more tears. At the hospital she had hardly been able to believe that Peggy was dead, but now, as her realization of the truth became stronger, utter desolation enveloped and overwhelmed her.

All thoughts of Clive and June had been temporarily displaced.

Christine kept appearing, though, in Caroline's mind. Not that the young girl was ever out of her thoughts for very long—but why now? Why was Christine there when there should only be room for Peggy?

Caroline deliberated on this for some time. She decided that Christine and Peggy had suffered in a strangely similar way. In both their bodies something had been growing—unwanted and threatening. Peggy's first cancer, just like Christine's baby, had had to be removed—torn from the female anatomy where it had been developing in warmth and safety.

Caroline halted this incongruous train of

thought. She should not draw such similarities, not between a malignant growth and an unborn child. She must get a grip on herself or she would go mad.

CHAPTER TWENTY-ONE

As she sat alone, the regrets and the guilt, which Caroline had postponed earlier, invaded her grief and heightened the anguish that she felt might send her out of her mind.

That morning, when she had turned away from Peggy ... it must have been then that her friend had found the lump. That anxious smile had been a plea for help. Peggy had needed someone to talk to and Caroline had turned her back. Now, to think of that moment was like taking a knife to her own heart. If only she had responded to Peggy . . . if only . . . Caroline was devoured by guilt once again ... a most dreadful guilt. If she had comforted her friend, as she had done before, perhaps Peggy would be alive now. Caroline was certain that she could have persuaded her to have treatment.

Poor, dear Peggy; what torment she must have suffered, and feeling that she could not confide in her best friend must have distressed her even more—and all because of a stupid argument!

Caroline thought back over the years. From the moment that she and Clive had moved into their house, she and Peggy had been friends. When the children were small, they had shared the anxieties and the joys which young mothers experience. Then, as their offspring had gained independence, they had found more time on their hands to simply enjoy each other's company. Caroline's married life would have been far more lonely and cheerless if Peggy had not been her close and dependable friend.

She and Peggy had always been there for each other whenever help or support was wanted. Except now, when Peggy had needed her most of all. This time Caroline had let her down. And now Peggy was dead. How could she live with this? How could she go on?

For the first time in her life, Caroline seriously contemplated suicide. She thought of the complete peace, the end of all earthly misery. It seemed the only way out. As she took her Valium from her bag, she saw, in her mind's eye, the empty pill bottles by Peggy's bed. She shuddered violently. She held the tablets tightly in her hand and, staring at the small, white tranquilizers, she considered how easy it would be. Then she thought of Peggy, lying dead, and she pushed the pills hurriedly back out of sight. No. Peggy had not looked peaceful. Caroline had seen no serenity, no dignity, in her death.

Perhaps dying in torment, and by one's own hand, would mean eternal torment . . . who could tell?

Caroline would not take that route. She did not know what she could do, or how she would manage, but she could not and would not take her own life.

Maybe she would be able to make amends, at least in part, for the dreadful thing she had done. She could be of practical help to Steven and the twins for a start. Peggy would have liked that.

Caroline sighed deeply. The first task, which seemed insurmountable, was to find a way of coping with the grief and remorse, which now held her heart and mind in their pitiless black grip.

*   *   *

Caroline still sat staring into the fire when Clive arrived home.

'Clive,' she began feebly, as he entered the lounge, 'bad news . . . terrible news . . . Peggy's dead.'

Clive dropped his briefcase onto a chair and looked at his wife.

'Good God . . . how?' his voice betraycd the shock that his face denied.

'She took an overdose.'

'Well! I'd never have thought that Peggy was the type to commit suicide! She was always so

180

cheerful. It just shows you, people are a real mystery sometimes; you think you know them, but . . .'

'She found another lump.'

'Oh . . . I see. How awful.' Clive poured his customary whisky before continuing. 'If she thought she was on the way out anyway, though, I suppose you can understand it.'

'But she could have been cured!'

'Maybe. We shall never know now, shall we?'

'But . . .'

Clive turned on the television.

'Clive . . .' Caroline continued, dismay evident in her voice. 'Don't you think that you should go next door and see how Steven's doing?'

He seemed to consider this suggestion deeply for a moment.

'Yes, I will. After dinner.'

'I haven't cooked any bloody dinner!'

Caroline's anger momentarily eased her grief.

'Oh.'

'Clive . . .' Caroline starting crying hysterically. 'I found her . . . I tried to save her . . . I feel sick with guilt because I made it impossible for her to talk to me this morning . . . I've lost my best friend! Peggy is dead! I didn't give a thought to your damned dinner!'

'Er . . . no . . . no, of course you didn't. Sorry. Don't worry; I'll go to the Chinese. Do you want anything? Spare ribs?'

Caroline could find no answer. She slowly shook her head and watched in amazement as Clive left the house. Was this man human? Did he have no feelings?

In that moment, Caroline's guilt drained entirely away from her. What had she been thinking of? It was not until she had witnessed Clive's reaction to the news of Peggy's death that she realized where the blame should really be placed.

It was all Clive's fault!

She and Peggy had never argued before, not until that day of their trip to London, and why had they rowed then? Because of Clive bloody Marshall and his floozy! If it had not been for his contemptible behaviour, Peggy would never have had to make the decision to keep quiet about the whole filthy business!

Clive had not only brought utter misery to Caroline because of the affair, but he had caused the rift between her and Peggy and, therefore, he must take responsibility for Peggy's suicide.

Caroline breathed heavily. She stared, with wide eyes, straight ahead. If anyone had been there to see her, they would have said that she looked insane, but Caroline would have argued that she was saner now than she had been for years. Because, as she thought over all that had happened, she found herself centralizing all blame for everything on Clive.

182

If he had agreed to have her mother live with them, she would be alive now. It was not Caroline's fault that she had neglected to talk her mother into entering an old people's home; she had always known that the old lady would have been very unhappy with such a suggestion. If Clive had allowed her to live with them, she would have felt wanted, and she could have spent her remaining years happy and contented. Instead, he would not have it. No . . . it was Clive's fault that her mother had died as she had.

Then there was Christine, the poor girl. When Caroline had learned of Adam's treatment of her, then heard her son's hard and uncaring views on the matter, she had realized that it was Clive's influence that had caused Adam to behave as he had done. Just as it was acceptable for Clive to treat her and June—yes—she knew that he had not treated June well either—in the degrading way he had done, so it was perfectly acceptable for his son to behave in that depraved manner. This had resulted in an abortion, the death of a child. Yes, just as long as Adam enjoyed his sexual exploits, it was all right for him to treat girls like dirt. That was how Clive obviously thought, and he had passed his smutty attitude on to his son. He would not even consider giving Christine a home so that she could keep her baby—his grandson.

Now that Clive had finally destroyed

183

Caroline's love for him, she could see clearly all that had evolved because of him and his arrogant, selfish ways.

It was unbearably tragic that it had taken Peggy's death to bring Caroline to her senses. She would never forgive Clive for anything— not now—not ever! And for Peggy's sake, she would make him understand exactly what he had done.

*　　　*　　　*

The next few days found Caroline too involved in helping Steven and the twins to take much notice of Clive. She still slept in the spare room, and she did not speak to him about their future. In fact, she barely uttered a word in his presence.

Steven and the boys were living in a daze, but Caroline could at least make sure that there was food on the table if they wanted it. This simple work, the shopping and cooking, did little to ease her own sorrow, but she was doing it for Peggy.

Each time she returned to her own home and looked at Clive, her revulsion grew. He seemed so unaware of all that he had done, but he would know. If there were any justice in this world, he would pay!

'Peggy's funeral's on Thursday,' Caroline announced sharply to Clive on Tuesday evening.

'I won't be able to come, Caro,' was the swift reply. 'We've got the auditors coming in—it's impossible.'

'Of course it is. Just remind me not to die when the auditors are due, will you? I'd hate you to miss my funeral!'

'Caro . . . !'

She was gone from the room.

CHAPTER TWENTY-TWO

Though it was still only February, the day of Peggy's funeral was sunny and mild. Since the one and only fall of snow, the weather had become gradually warmer. The first tiny buds were appearing on the trees and the days were growing a little longer. Large clusters of purple and yellow crocuses in the churchyard drew everyone's attention, their brightness seeming inappropriate for such a sad occasion.

Peggy's relatives surrounded Steven and the twins, as though protecting them from any contact with the outside world. Caroline stood alone in the church. Her eyes seemed fixed on the coffin; Peggy was dead, gone forever. She cried hot, salty tears for her friend.

Sorrow had been her constant companion for so long that it seemed natural for Caroline to feel unhappy. She had even stopped wondering if joy would ever return to her life.

She no longer expected it to.

*   *   *

The days following the funeral found Caroline's all-consuming hatred for Clive growing with each hour that passed. She could not bear to be in his company. They no longer seemed able to communicate, even about the most mundane of matters.

The resolution she had made to stay with him was one she now found quite impossible to keep. She did not want to part, though, until she had made him feel some responsibility for the misery and suffering he had caused. Clive would never feel guilt; Caroline was certain that it was not present in his repertoire of emotions. But surely he could be made to understand that he was to blame for so much distress. He should not be allowed to live his life in complete ignorance of his own plentiful flaws and dire mistakes.

Her absolute abhorrence of her husband was becoming an obsession, and Caroline's rationality was adversely affected by its intensity. The search for a way to force Clive into some sort of realization of his sins became a pressing cause, which, at least, provided her with something other than grief to concentrate on.

CHAPTER TWENTY-THREE

The first Saturday in March found Clive in his garden. It was sunny, and spring was prematurely in the air.

Caroline stood working at the kitchen window. As she prepared the vegetables for lunch, she watched with contempt as Clive scrubbed the winter's grime from the fountain. He then inspected the spring bulbs that would soon be in flower.

'Making sure the daffodils are in straight lines, no doubt,' Caroline muttered sarcastically.

Next, the stepladder was brought out, and the electric hedge cutter.

'Yes,' thought Caroline, 'I can see at least half a dozen twigs just protruding from that hedge. We can't have that, can we? Let's get our priorities right. We must attend to what is truly important in our lives!'

Clive stood the stepladder up next to the pond. He began eyeing the hedge and trimming it where he deemed it necessary.

'He'll put a spirit level on that bloody privet in a minute,' Caroline pondered. She collected the vegetable peelings and went out to dispose of them.

'What colour shall we do the inside of the pool—the walls and so on?' Clive called, as though there were no possibility that Caroline might be about to leave him.

'Black,' was the terse response.

'Are you serious?'

'Deadly. It suits my mood.'

Clive sighed.

'Oh dear—what is it today—Peggy? Or is it me again—the wicked husband?'

'Both.'

Caroline wandered over to the pond.

'It's no good brooding over things, Caro,' Clive said, moving the stepladder along so that he could reach a wayward twig.

'So I've been told.'

'I'm not going to spend the rest of my life apologizing, if that's what you think. I've said I'm sorry—I can't undo what happened.'

'I hate this garden,' Caroline announced, clearly unimpressed by what her husband was saying.

'What?'

'I do. I loathe and detest it.'

'Why, for God's sake?' Clive looked injured.

'You wouldn't understand if I tried to explain,' Caroline replied vaguely.

'Oh, too clever for me now, are you?'

'Yes, Clive. Granted, not as far as money is concerned; I'll give you that. If it's banking or insurance or unit shares or whatever, I bow to your superior knowledge; but anything else, Clive—anything of real importance—you're utterly stupid.'

'Am I, indeed?'

'Have you heard of Oscar Wilde, Clive?'

'Of course I've heard of Oscar Wilde!'

'He talked about people who know the price of everything and the value of nothing. You're one of those people, Clive—it's sad, really.'

Clive, who was at the top of the stepladder, turned to deliver a caustic reply to his wife, when he over-balanced. The ladder wobbled and he dropped the hedge-cutter into the pond.

'Oh, hell!' he snapped. 'Now look what you've made me do! Turn the switch off on the patio, will you.'

Caroline did just that.

As Clive leaned over the side of the stepladder to retrieve the cutter from the pond, Caroline could see, quite clearly, that pig of a man lying in the arms of his mistress. She could see Peggy's face, ashen and ugly and dying. Then her mother's kind old face was there, as it had been when she was lying in hospital, her death imminent. Christine's baby—that ghastly dream—it was all there. These things simultaneously collided in her brain. Her heart swelled with a hatred so vicious that she thought she would choke. As her mind erupted with the injustice of it all, Clive put his hand in the water. In that instant, Caroline turned on the electricity.

She watched dispassionately as the current passed through his body. His bolting eyes met hers, and in the final few seconds of their marriage—and of his life—both Clive and Caroline knew who was triumphant. He lurched violently and fell from the steps; his head hit the stone fish fountain. Caroline heard the crack. Then he sprawled face down in the pond and lay perfectly still, the lifeless fish spraying water gently onto his broken skull.

Caroline went into the house and took off her rubber gloves. She put on her coat and walked to the shops.

*   *   *

The sun felt quite warm on her face as Caroline reached the parade. Her head was held high, her step was light and she felt absolutely contented.

'Will you have any litters of puppies in the near future?' she asked the man in the pet shop.

'Yes, there are some golden Labradors coming in. They've just been born so it'll be six to eight weeks before they can leave their mother.'

'Ok, I'll have one of them. I've been promising myself a puppy for a long time now.'

'Right, ma'am. You'll see when they're in, if you pass this way.'

Caroline smiled broadly, her eyes twinkling.

'I'll keep my eyes open. Thank you.'

190

She cheerily greeted several of her neighbours as she enjoyed her long stroll around the town. After an hour or so, she arrived back home. An ambulance and a police car stood outside her house. Someone had saved her the trouble of calling them.

Now the act must begin.

*   *   *

'Caroline!' Steven's voice rang out as he rushed along the front path to meet her. 'Caroline . . . something dreadful has happened!'

'What, Steven? What is it?' she asked, her acting abilities showing much promise. Steven led her into the lounge and made her sit down.

'It's Clive,' he replied as gently as he could, 'there's been an accident, a terrible accident.'

'What do you mean 'an accident'? What's happened?' Caroline found the look of panic comparatively simply to feign; it had been her most faithful companion in recent months.

'I was bringing back the casserole dish—the one you brought the stew in . . .'

'Yes?'

'And . . . I found Clive . . . in the garden.'

'What's wrong with him?'

'Caroline . . . there's no easy way to tell you this . . . I'm sorry, but Clive's dead.'

'Dead? In the garden? But how . . . what . . .'

'I'm sorry, Caroline.'

191

A pause in the proceedings seemed fitting here. Caroline hung her head and wished that she did not have to wait so long for a puppy.

'What was it, Steven . . . a heart attack?' she asked, her voice quivering impressively.

'No, he fell off the stepladder and into the pond.'

'Yes, I remember . . . you said it was an accident . . . I can't seem to think straight.'

'It seems that he cracked his head on the fountain . . . the stone fish.'

'That was his pride and joy—he loved his garden very much.'

'I'm so sorry, Caroline. I don't know what else to say, but I do know exactly how you feel.' Steven put a comforting arm around her shoulders.

'I can't cry, Steven,' she whispered. 'Why can't I cry?'

'It's shock . . . some people react that way. I'll pour you a whisky.'

As she sipped the drink, a policeman entered the room.

'Mrs. Marshall?' he said, kindly.

'Yes.'

'Your neighbour has told you what happened?'

She nodded her head slowly.

'They're taking your husband now, Mrs. Marshall. I don't advise it, but if you do want to . . .'

'No . . . no, I don't, thank you . . . I can't

look at him . . . not yet, anyway.'

The policeman nodded to someone in the hall and a few seconds later the ambulance pulled away.

'It looks like it was the blow that killed him, Mrs. Marshall, but the post-mortem will tell us for certain. The power to the hedge-cutter was turned on, you see—so the electrified water might have caused heart failure. Like dropping a hair-drying in the bath.'

'It doesn't really matter what caused it, does it? He's gone; that's the only thing that matters.'

'I'm sorry, Mrs. Marshall. It's all very sad.'

'Poor Clive,' Caroline muttered, attempting to bring forth tears.

'You left your husband gardening when you went out, Mrs. Marshall?'

'Yes . . . yes, he said he'd be tidying up out there while I went to the shops.'

'It's a very secluded garden, isn't it? The hedges are high on both sides.'

'Yes, Clive liked it that way.'

'Well, I don't expect we'll need to talk to you again, Mrs. Marshall,' the policeman said sombrely as he turned to leave. 'Will you be all right now?'

'Yes . . . I think so . . . yes. Thank you. Goodbye.'

Steven returned to Caroline's side.

'We're in the same boat, you and I,' he sympathized gently.

'Yes, I suppose we are.' Caroline finished her whisky. 'We've had our disagreements, Clive and I,' she explained, 'well . . . you know, don't you?'

Steven nodded.

'But I did love him, Steven. I truly did.'

The two of them sat in silence for some time. Caroline wished that Steven would go; it was becoming a strain to keep up the false grief.

*   *   *

Adam was sent for. He arrived home late at night, shocked and very subdued. He and his mother sat up talking until the early hours. Caroline wanted desperately to sleep, but she knew that it was therapeutic for Adam to talk about Clive, so she could not be selfish enough to deny him her company. Especially as it was she who had deprived him of his father.

'For someone like dad,' Adam said, 'to be snuffed out so suddenly . . . I still can't believe it, mum . . . not really.'

'Any death is dreadful, Adam.'

'Yes, I know, but dad was so . . . so strong and clever and . . . he was just brilliant!' Suddenly Adam sounded like a little boy again.

'So that's how you saw him,' Caroline whispered to herself.

'When I was a kid—still at school—and we used to go to the cricket together, he used to

194

talk to me a lot. Especially about his own father.'

'That's odd; he rarely mentioned his parents to me.'

'He loved his dad very much. I suppose it was because his mother died first. The two of them had a few years on their own after she'd gone. He used to tell me how proud he was of his dad, what with him being a miner. He often said he wished that I'd known my Grandad Marshall. He showed me the old chap's Davy-lamp once.'

'I didn't know all that. I didn't even know he'd still got his dad's Davy-lamp.'

'Oh, yes, it's in that little wooden chest in the garage; he keeps . . . kept it . . . locked.'

'I wondered what was in there—I thought it was full of girly magazines.'

'He was only young when his dad died, wasn't he?'

'About sixteen, I think. He went to live with an aunt. She died just after you were born.'

'He had that awful thing miners get, didn't he? Coal dust in the lungs?'

'Yes; it must have been a terrible illness.'

'Dad told me how he watched his father waste away . . . turn from a big, healthy man to skin and bone. Most of the time it was dad who looked after him, apparently—him and the district nurse. He said that towards the end, his breathing was so laboured that he could hardly whisper.'

'How dreadful.'

'Can you imagine fighting like that for every breath? Dad sat and held his hand when he was dying. He said it was like touching a skeleton. Poor dad. He never got over it, you know, watching his father die slowly like that.'

'No . . . I can imagine how that kind of experience would make a lasting impression on someone so young.'

'He said to me that as he watched his dad gasping his last breath, he promised himself he would never go through that kind of pain again. That's why he sometimes seemed a bit hard, I suppose. He was afraid to love anyone too much—afraid of the pain that comes with real love. I think he tried to keep us all at arm's length . . . did you feel like that?'

'Yes, Adam,' Caroline replied in an undertone, but with conviction. 'I did.'

*   *   *

Early next morning, Caroline took Clive's bunch of keys and went to the garage. She found the one that fitted the little wooden chest. There, inside, was the Davy lamp and an old watch—that must have been his father's, too.

'Why couldn't you have shared it with me, Clive?' she uttered tearfully. 'Perhaps I could have understood, if you'd told me about your pain.'

Those were the only genuine tears that Caroline would ever cry for Clive. She could not allow herself to become sentimental—not now. The idea of a loving, caring Clive must be expunged from her mind.

For God's sake, she reasoned, if he had learned so much about love and pain at sixteen years old, he should have been more sensitive to the plight of others, not less! No, there must be no excuse for what he had done. There could be none—it was too late.

*　　　*　　　*

A verdict of accidental death was returned by the coroner a few days later. Caroline was comforted by one and all as the grieving widow.

CHAPTER TWENTY-FOUR

Standing in church, at her third funeral in the space of a few months, Caroline's face appeared tortured and desolate, but her heart was exhilarated.

She felt no guilt—absolutely none. Although she had murdered her husband, Caroline was experiencing true peace of mind for the first time in years.

She had done it for Peggy, for her mother,

for Christine and her baby, but most of all . . . for herself.

Caroline wondered if June would be grieving for Clive; she hoped so. Oh, she really hoped so!

Adam was still very distressed about his father's death, but he would soon recover—the young always do. Caroline was pleased to see him go back to Cambridge. She did not want him around her—not any more.

Clive, being a man of some financial expertise, had insured both himself and Caroline very wisely. She would have no money worries at all, and she would be able to keep her home. He owed her that much. In his will, it was stipulated that Adam should receive the small, wooden chest and its contents. Clive had also invested some money for his son.

*　　*　　*

Caroline found life on her own to be surprisingly enjoyable. She got up when she wished, ate what she wanted when she felt like it, and generally grew accustomed to her freedom. For so long she had avoided life as a single woman. If only she had known of the rewards that such an existence could offer! She no longer wore layers of make-up; there was no need to hide her imperfections, not any more, and her hair was no longer styled and sprayed. She would let it grow and hang loosely around her shoulders. She was her own woman now; she would do as she wished. The only thing that the independent Caroline truly missed was sex. In moments of stark self-honesty, she had to admit that she needed a physical relationship—with whom, though? There was no one.

Occasionally, Caroline wondered if she was insane. If anyone had told her a year ago that she would be a murderess, she would have believed him or her to be out of their mind. Now, though . . . now that she had committed that most notorious of crimes, she felt completely at ease about it. If she was insane, it was quite wonderful. She decided that she had no wish to return to her previous chaotic state of mind. If that was sanity, she had finished with it.

*   *   *

Every time she walked past Maison June, Caroline held her head up high, but she never looked in. She knew that she was afraid to face the wretched woman, and though this bothered her, she decided to keep her dead husband's mistress at a safe distance. June had other ideas, however. One morning, as Caroline passed the salon, the hairdresser rushed out and stood in front of her, looking her squarely in the eyes.

'I must speak to you,' June exclaimed with some urgency.

'Must you? Really?'

'Look, I know that you must hate me, and I can understand that . . .'

'Yes, I hate you,' Caroline answered, with vitriolic clarity. She felt far calmer, faced with this woman, than she had imagined she would. 'But I doubt if you understand at all.'

'No . . . well . . . I just wanted to tell you that Clive loved you, not me. It was just sex with us, that's all—a bit of fun. It was you that he really cared about. Now that he's dead, I wanted to make sure you knew that; I thought it might help you to cope with your loss.'

'Did you?' Caroline roared, causing passers-by to stare inquiringly in her direction. 'Well, it doesn't help one little bit! In fact, it makes everything ten times worse!'

'What? I don't understand . . .'

'No, your sort never does! To be honest, June, I couldn't be less concerned about who Clive loved or didn't love. What matters to me, is that I stopped loving him, and I'm not a grieving widow, either—I'm having the time of my life! What your bit of fun did do though was—albeit indirectly—to cause the death of a woman whose name I wouldn't sully by speaking it in your presence!'

A small crowd was gathering. June looked embarrassed. Caroline did not.

'What? Whose death? What are you talking

about?'

'She didn't even die because of a great love between you, apparently! No—it was just a bit of fun! You're filth, June, nothing more than filth! And don't try salving your guilty conscience on me again!'

Caroline walked straight ahead, as though June, who had to hop smartly to one side, was not there.

That afternoon, Caroline went to the crematorium. She placed spring flowers on her mother's grave, and on Peggy's. On Clive's she laid a large weed from his garden; it seemed appropriate and enormously satisfying.

*　　　*　　　*

About a month after Clive's death, the airline tickets arrived for the holiday in Venice, which they had planned for the end of April. Caroline deliberated what she should do.

Predictably, Mrs. Curran urged her to go and enjoy herself, saying that Clive would not have wanted her to miss her holiday because of him.

Caroline smiled feebly, as though reluctant to be persuaded. Venice in the spring did sound very tempting, but she did not really want to go alone. If only she could have taken Peggy . . . Caroline forced back the grief, which still surged through her whenever she thought of her dear, dead, friend.

'I know!' she declared, searching through her handbag and extracting a crumpled piece of paper. She dialled the number scribbled on it. 'Christine?' she said. 'It's Caroline Marshall—Adam's mum. I don't know if you've heard, dear, but Mr. Marshall is dead ... there was an accident.'

'Oh, no! I'm so sorry,' came the stunned reply. 'I didn't know—I don't see Adam now.'

'It happened a few weeks ago; it was all very sudden. Anyway, what I really wanted to know was, would you like to come on holiday to Italy with me? I'd forgotten all about it, to tell you the truth, but the tickets for Venice arrived this morning, and . . . well . . . there's one spare now. I wondered if you'd like to go?'

'Er . . . I don't know what to say! . . . It's all so unexpected!'

'Yes, it is a bit, isn't it?' Caroline giggled. 'We were due to go two weeks on Saturday—what do you think?'

'What about Annabel?'

'Annabel?'

'Yes—the baby.'

Caroline paused. For a second she did not understand.

'I'm sorry, Christine,' she said, 'do you mean you had the baby?'

'Didn't Adam tell you?'

'No, he didn't.'

'He only phoned me once, and that was ages ago, but I did tell him that I was definitely going ahead with the pregnancy.'

'He didn't say anything,' Caroline muttered, still in shock. 'And I phoned your home a few days after you'd left here. Your mother said you were staying with friends . . . so I thought that meant you had gone for the abortion.'

'Yes, I did plan to, but I couldn't go through with it when the time came.'

'Does Adam know that he has a daughter?'

'No, he's never contacted me apart from that one call. I was only three or four months pregnant then, so, as he never tried to find out whether it was a boy or a girl, I took it that he wasn't interested.'

'He didn't try to find out about the baby at all? He might be my son, Christine, but he's a mystery to me, he really is. Not interested, eh? Heartless swine! Well, I am interested in her!' Caroline was becoming excited. 'I'll phone the airline tomorrow and we'll book Annabel a seat—that's if we need to—and we'll take her to Italy with us!'

'Ok,' agreed Christine. 'Why not?'

'I'll let you know the details soon . . . bye, Christine.'

Caroline sat down, and allowed the thought that she had a grandchild to penetrate. She felt elated.

So, she reflected, Clive had not been responsible for a baby's death. Then, quickly changing tack, she reminded herself that it was no thanks to Clive that the child was still

203

alive—it was only Christine's feminine conscience that had saved Annabel. Now that Caroline had found her way—her strength—nothing she learned about Clive would cause the old self-doubts to return—nothing.

*　　*　　*

Over the next two weeks, as Caroline prepared for her holiday, she found it difficult to maintain the depressing air of widowhood.

'Will you and the boys be all right while I'm away?' she asked Steven, just a day or two before she was due to leave.

'Thanks, Caroline, we'll be fine. Don't you dare worry about us while you're in Venice!'

'Steven,' Caroline began hesitantly, 'you don't think that people will consider me heartless, do you? Going to Italy when Clive's only been dead a few weeks.'

'Of course not! The holiday will do you the world of good, and everyone who knows you will say the same!'

'It was planned ages ago. Clive took care of that kind of thing.'

'Look, a break is just what you need. Everyone will understand, and if they don't— they aren't worth bothering about.'

Caroline smiled. She had felt that she should make some show of conscience about her trip, and that being done, she was ready for the off.

The evening before she flew out, Caroline phoned Adam in Cambridge.

'I'm off to Venice tomorrow,' she announced, somewhat abruptly.

'Yes . . . of course . . . you and dad were going, weren't you?'

'That's right, only now I'm going with Christine. You remember Christine Jordan, don't you?' There was silence for a few seconds. 'We're taking your daughter, Annabel, with us. I know that you have no interest in the child, but as I'm about to fly off to Italy with her, I thought it an opportune moment to tell you that I know of her existence.'

'Yes, well . . . I've been busy lately, mum. I haven't had time to . . .'

'No, of course not—busy with your studies, eh?' Caroline interrupted. 'Don't work too hard, will you? Bye!'

Adam was shocked. His mother was glad.

*   *   *

Caroline met Christine and the baby at the airport. Annabel was delightful; she slept soundly in her grandmother's arms until they landed in Italy. It was wonderful for Caroline to hold a tiny baby again. She could see that

205

Annabel bore a strong resemblance to Adam, but thought it wise not to mention that.

CHAPTER TWENTY-FIVE

Venice was warm and welcoming. Its unique beauty was everything that Caroline had hoped it would be, and the hotel was excellent.

The two women shared the chores that a baby creates, and the holiday was a great success. They took several gondola trips, so that they could savour, and commit to memory, the strange quaintness of the canals with their low bridges and bizarre traffic. It was all so relaxing. Sometimes they would browse around the shops, choosing souvenirs or buying presents for Annabel. They found charming gardens too, where they could simply sit and take in the colour and scent of the magnificent spring blooms. Time passed too quickly.

On the morning before they were due to fly home, they stood in Saint Marco Square.

'I wish we could stay here,' Christine sighed.

'Me too,' Caroline sighed back, before taking advantage of the moment.

'Christine,' she said, 'I don't quite know how to say this . . . but I've gathered that things aren't easy for you at home, with your mother's arthritis and everything.' Caroline's concern was obvious.

'No, it's all a bit tense. The house is so small; we seem to be under each other's feet all the time. There's so much paraphernalia with a baby.'

'As you know, I'm on my own now. I've got loads of room, so why don't you come and live with me? You and Annabel. We could try it and see how it works out, anyway.'

'Yes, I suppose we could do that. We've got on well so far, haven't we?'

'That's what I thought. And you could still see your parents as much as you like, couldn't you?'

'It's very tempting. You've got such a lovely house and a very big garden for Annabel to play in when she gets older.'

'Is that a "yes", then? Shall we give it a try?'

'Yes . . . yes. All right. We'll give it a try.'

Caroline kissed Christine's cheek. The girl smelled hot and sensuous. Her skin was tanned now, and she looked quite beautiful. Caroline thought that her son was a fool.

*   *   *

With Christine and Annabel in the house, Caroline was ecstatic. She woke each morning looking forward to a day of companionship from Christine, and the sheer joy of watching her granddaughter grow.

The two women lived in total harmony;

neither one bearing any anxiety that they might upset the other. They were able to be themselves—there was no pretence.

In the evenings, when Annabel had been bathed and taken to bed, smelling sweetly of talcum powder and that special warm baby aroma, the women would sit together and share their peace. Sometimes they would talk, but if they were silent, it did not matter; they were too close, by now, for conversation to be a necessity. Often, Caroline would read while Christine made tiny clothes for her daughter. Life was serene.

Neither of the women were gardeners, so Clive's previously perfect garden took on a far more natural look. This afforded Caroline great pleasure. She hoped that, if there was a heaven, and he had, by some divine error, been admitted, Clive would be looking down horrified by the sight of weeds growing in his flowerbeds and a rarely mowed lawn.

Adam came to visit occasionally. He sometimes brought a present for Annabel, but he never stayed for very long. His mother and ex-lover were both relieved about that.

Caroline, in particular, found Adam's visits rather disconcerting. She resented his presence and, though she told no one, she felt strangely jealous when he talked to Christine. Once, it seemed like centuries ago now, Caroline had wanted Adam and Christine to marry. Now, the thought of them being together was repugnant to her. Christine had become such an important part of her life, that Caroline wanted to share her with no one; except Annabel, of course. Caroline felt very protective towards the girl, and she did not want Adam around.

Although she was busy with the baby, Caroline still helped Steven and the twins, though not as much as before. All three males were becoming quite proficient cooks and housemaids. Occasionally, if Christine and Caroline wanted to go to the cinema, Steven and the boys would baby-sit for them. It pleased Caroline to see how Annabel brought joy to Peggy's family.

*   *   *

'You know that shell of a swimming pool?' Caroline said one evening soon after Annabel's first birthday.

'What about it?'

'Why don't we have the pool part filled in and make it into a huge playroom for Annabel? And her friends too, as she gets older. We could even have a playgroup in there—it's big enough.'

'That would be marvellous!'

'I'm going to get rid of that damned fountain. And the pond, too.'

'Good idea. I hate that stone fish.'

'Do you? I feel rather sorry for it.'

209

Christine grinned. 'Yes,' she said, 'it can't be much fun, standing out in that pond in all weathers.'

'I've always wanted a puppy,' Caroline went on wistfully. 'I was going to get one a while back, but what with the baby and everything . . .'

'Oh, let's get one!' Christine pleaded. 'I love dogs. Annabel and the pup could grow up together.'

'Right, you're on. Potty training and puppy training, here we come! Do you think we'll be able to cope?'

'Definitely!'

*   *   *

In the June of their second summer together, the relationship between Caroline and Christine developed into a physical one. This had not been planned, but both women felt fulfilled and united by their joy in each other's affection.

They had both been hurt—terribly hurt by men they had loved, and neither one would ever feel secure in such a relationship again. In each other they found confidence, strength and absolute devotion. There would never be any more doubt.

Caroline and Christine made no secret of their relationship. They were not ashamed of their mutual love. The few friends that they had, accepted their way of life completely, and these were the only people whose opinion the couple valued anyway.

Adam's visits, however, became extremely infrequent when he learned of their lesbian relationship. Caroline and Christine decided that this was his problem, and gave the subject no more thought.

*   *   *

So Caroline found true happiness for the first time in her life. She had lied and murdered to achieve this idyllic state, but that was a secret that would die with her. Now, she scarcely thought about it; she was far too busy.

*   *   *

As she carried Annabel into the garden one perfect, sunny afternoon, Caroline said to the baby:

'We're going to get some men to dig up this garden, Annabel. And we're going to plant hundreds of flowers, so that we'll have our very own meadow. We'll have cornflowers, poppies, larkspurs, all kinds of lovely things, and you can watch the beautiful butterflies when they come each summer. Won't that be wonderful, darling? Our very own meadow.'

Caroline kissed Annabel.

'Mary, Mary, quite contrary,' she whispered. 'How does your garden grow?'